THORNE

THE ESSENCE CHRONICLES

THORNE

HAYLEY GABRIELLE

CONTENTS

ONE

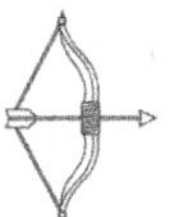

THE MOON GLITTERED AND SHONE IN THE water, its splendour mirrored there amongst stars bright enough to turn any ordinary human near blind. But Thorne was no ordinary human, and often he would stand for hours at the cliff face to revel in the beauty of the night.

It was, in part, to escape any excessive interaction with the other Essences, though he also considered it his duty to appreciate a land he had been granted. A land that was as much *his* as it was anyone else's, considering the humans could only really take Pride in it with Thorne's assistance. His lips curled at the thought.

Over all the years the Overseer had permitted free will, Thorne had been labelled many things—Hauteur, Arrogance, Conceit, Vanity—but he was more than any word. He was a swinging pendulum on a scale set by Good and Evil. However the closest he had heard them come to pinning him into a series of letters—though he knew it was derisible child's play to do so—was *Pride*.

He was Pride in all manner of things. Every human desired to feel some degree of self-worth, and he made it possible. He was caught in the breath of romantic introduction, the rise of a chin accepting a challenge, the tears a mother shed watching her children grow. He was essential for the human experience, and that pleased him greatly.

The other Essences … they played a part too, though seemed to possess far less awareness of social norms. Thorne was as much a singularity as they were, but Pride was not so cataclysmically irritating, in his opinion.

On this night, he was to cut his night walk short. There was somewhere else he had to be. Someone important he'd agreed to meet.

His smooth, ebony hair glinted midnight blue under the moon as he raked a hand through it. The air smelt of sweet fields of flowers and sea salt and he drank it in one last time with his eyes drawn shut.

Thorne was constructed by a divine hand. His body emulated that of a human, but it was not the same. Nor would he want it to be. All that was tangible or mundane did not touch him. Or the other Essences, he begrudgingly admitted to himself. The heart did not *need* to beat, the eyes see, the fingers touch or the nose smell. Not for him. All of it was a gift; token recompense for existing void of the human spirit.

Though he never particularly desired to exist as humans did. He still had choice—fluctuating between what humans liked to call *right* or *wrong*—and that was enough. It was more than enough.

Thorne drew back from the landscape and cast himself into the ethereal curtain behind all that was living, in a burst of spectacular emerald light.

He swept like a glorious wraith through the darkness, following a trail he knew all too well. Spirals of colour rushed by, amethyst waves dancing closer than the rest. He continued on and did his best to ignore them. Sometimes, if he were to think too deeply about an Essence, they'd appear before him as if he'd begged a question and they'd arrived to answer it. He shook his head, recalling all those uninvited visits sparked by simply pondering one of his friends a little too long.

The colours shredded back to darkness and he landed gracefully atop the highest tower of Rylora, the jewel of the northern continent.

It was an elegant city built amidst expansive opal mining caves. Thorne often shifted there to admire its construction—the walls rocky and untouched, each roof sanded flat and polished to reveal glittering, imbedded opals. They reflected the sun like wildfire during the day and during the night, as they did now under his feet, echoed the moon's angelic radiance.

The land of Rylora bordered with Lockmill, home to a fierce throng of people forever intent on battle and expansion. Lockmill's poor, paranoid neighbour to the east, the region of Thanron, lived in constant fear of invasion and raids. But Rylora ... they were too strong to be a target for

Lockmill. And they knew it.

The moon shot iridescent flares across the glimmering opal roofs, setting them alight as Thorne shifted to the lower balcony of Pacer Barlon's sleeping quarters.

The ruler of Rylora was waiting for him there in a royal blue nightgown, his elbows resting on the polished ivory railing as he looked out upon the courtyard. A wall fountain of peridot and iridescent yellow circled the entire space. Sheets of water cut down into a track running along the outer wall, the area paved apart from one exposed, central pool where the fountain's water collected in the outline of a quivering full moon.

"Admiring your handiwork?" Thorne said, balancing on the rail of the balcony.

The old man jolted in surprise. Then he recovered his composure with a wry smile and shifted his gaze to the vicinity of Thorne's voice.

"You take great pleasure in terrorising me with these unannounced greetings, don't you my friend?"

"How else am I supposed to announce my presence if not with a greeting?" Thorne posed.

Barlon held a finger decorated in rings of onyx mottled with opal up to his pursed lips. "Perhaps we can get you a bell."

Thorne raised a dark brow. Not many could get away with such a comment, but the pair had known each other since Pacer Barlon's induction, and while Thorne was invisible to the ruler, verbal teasing had become a standard mode of communication.

He jumped deftly to balcony level. "Only if you craft it from solid gold."

"I will inform my finest goldsmith," Pacer Barlon replied, a broad grin now showing within his frosted, cropped beard. "Until then, perhaps you could clear your throat from a few yards away before approaching."

"I'll consider it," Thorne allowed.

Barlon glanced back at his room, concealed by a thick, blue curtain. "You know, she was awake the last time we met," he whispered, presumably about his blaze—the woman asleep inside. "When I returned to bed she asked who I was speaking with, and I pretended I was caught in a dream." Barlon chuckled, stifling the sound with his hand. His nightgown shifted enough that the Insignia of Truth became visible against his skin, triangular with a horizontal line drawn threw it, glinting silver in the moonlight. "I spoke in riddles to convince her of it," continued Pacer Barlon, "and then I pretended to drift back into an undisturbed sleep."

Thorne's shoulders shook with silent laughter. "I'm torn between thanking you for upholding my secret or deeming you a bastard."

"Do both if you care to," Barlon said. "Perhaps I *am* a bastard for withholding the Truth from her."

"Don't be daft," Thorne sniped, his previously pleasant tone turning instantly sour. "It would be a severe betrayal."

Barlon pressed his fingers to the Insignia at his chest. "I know," he said softly, and then looked up at the night sky.

Thorne remained skeptical about Pacers knowing the Truth. Humans were undeniably fallible. They made rash decisions, particularly when they committed to a blaze and irrational emotions tended to cloud all logic.

One Pacer led every city or village cluster across Ethra, and the Overseer had some divine influence in the selection process. They were to know of the Essences in order to protect them and keep their people away from the Petrified Forest, where the oases—homes for the Essences—were hidden.

The highest level of secrecy was supposedly adhered to amongst the Pacers, and they were only to speak the Truth in the presence of those who knew it too—those also bearing the Insignia. But even then, such talk existed mostly in fleeting murmurs and hushed conversations behind closed doors.

"Have you given much thought to my proposal?" Barlon inquired, his eyes skirting the empty space holding his friend's disembodied voice.

Thorne sighed. "We exist in the Petrified Forest for a reason, Barlon." And yet if he were honest with himself, a part of him often fantasized about moving his oasis to Rylora's glistening, opal-bedecked terrain. Yet of course, it wasn't feasible.

"Rylora is where you belong!" Barlon threw up his hands. "It's where you exist *already* in immense proportions. My people are Proud, and that is only possible because of you. It seems only fitting you should reside amongst them."

Thorne winced. The notion did please him very much. "My answer remains the same," he said with no small degree of concerted effort. "I implore you not to tempt me further."

Releasing an exasperated breath, Pacer Barlon strode to the balcony's rail, his robe whispering against the tiles. "It's a shame, to design almost this entire city and then live so far from it."

Thorne smiled at that. When Rylora was first constructed, he had spent hours assisting the Pacer of the time with plans for the buildings and grounds. It was he that suggested flattening and polishing the roofs to display the opals in their full splendour.

"It takes me seconds to shift here," he said. "That will have to do."

"Well." Barlon shrugged. "The guest wing remains open to you. I keep it free of staff, just in case."

"I'm aware," Thorne crooned. "And I utilise the bedroom frequently."

"Oh?" Barlon turned and arched a greying brow.

Thorne winked, momentarily forgetting that his face was absent in the Pacer's mortal sight. He was struck, just for a second, by the sorrow of the fact that it always would be.

TWO

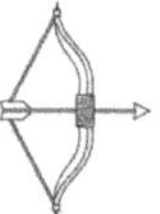

THORNE WAFTED INTO HIS BODY AS HE SWEPT up to the grand, oak door marking the entrance of his home. Intricate patterns were gilded into its surface, sweeping in arches and waves and skittering lines to represent the movement of his true form.

The oasis itself was set atop a steep hill nearby the shoreline—a tall, stone construction with a single tower and vaulted portico. Every angle, adornment, and precisely placed stone mirrored the sharp-edged planes of his human form. With a firm jaw and domineering cheekbones, he seemed almost a chiselled corner of his own stonework.

He sighed, recalling Pacer Barlon's offer to relocate. The idea was alluring. Though there was a charm about the coastline. A wild, unrestrained beauty. And Thorne was all three—charming, wild and beautiful. The sea mist and tranquility of the place could not be found elsewhere, and ultimately he knew he could not easily give it up.

Flinging his cloak over a velvet chaise, Thorne made for his bedroom on the second and top floor, which was no less grand than the rest of the house. A four-poster bed covered

in a silky maroon duvet occupied most of the space, a window overlooked his training ground and the coast beyond, and a ceiling-to-floor mirror covered the expansive back wall. The mirror offered the room an even greater sense of spacial luxury. Its purpose wasn't *solely* for superficial self-reflection, as Asha so often mused, but was a clever design strategy.

Thorne stripped to his undergarments and considered his muscular build in the mirror. His human body was sharp and defined, and he kept it that way with runs along the sand and combative training behind the house as often as he could. It was for his own benefit, considering most people in Ethra couldn't see so much as his fingertip. But he enjoyed remaining trim. He was gifted a body, and he would honour it.

"Ever the spectacle," a voice crooned from the doorway.

Thorne pivoted to see Harlie—Honesty embodied in a hawk-eyed, sandy-haired, slender female. Though irritated by her impromptu appearance, he was glad for the compliment, for Harlie could tell nothing but truths.

"Do you expect anything less?" he replied, unperturbed by her overt scrutiny of his bare torso.

"No," she said, those luminous eyes shifting down to his legs.

There was a time many centuries ago—while still fascinated by the physical abilities of their human forms—that Thorne and Harlie had engaged in some rather uncouth activities in that very room. The memories came back to Thorne as sharp and vivid as if they took place only yesterday.

Already curious as to the behaviour he'd come to learn whereby humans sought pleasure by almost whatever means possible, Thorne had wondered if perhaps he might also appreciate such intoxications.

It was the night Harlie had shifted into his home unannounced to find him utterly naked after a swim in the ocean, that they attempted it. She had first declared him to be *strikingly handsome by the average human's standard.* The comment had so moved him that he'd taken her to his bed. She didn't seem opposed, perhaps vaguely curious herself— and they had explored all bodily possibilities until dawn announced itself through the window.

The experience had been a little confusing, occasionally gratifying, and mostly awkward. Thorne decided that further practice was required, though it seemed Harlie would not persist.

"I cannot say I particularly cared for it," she had pronounced, once it was over. "You are far too heavy for someone of my size, and though there were moments of vague elation, I was considerably uncomfortable throughout most of it."

Heavy. The word had pierced Thorne's Pride as easily as a knife through butter. And when he had pointed out that his weight was purely attributable to muscle mass—she merely shrugged, and went on to critique every aspect of his performance.

This, of course, led to her expulsion from his home.

Everything about Harlie was sharp; from her aquiline nose and stiff shoulders to that wretched tongue capable of glowing declarations or utter slaughter.

It had taken Thorne five years to loosen his hold on the grudge preventing him from so much as glancing her way. Even during Breathings he would maintain his distance.

But in the end, he supposed, his Pride was too great to allow Harlie to dictate any lingering discontentment. After all, to become preoccupied by another's opinion was a relinquishing of power.

So he had chosen to leave the ordeal behind—and this was the first time she had set foot in his bedroom since that regrettable night.

"I have a door, you know," he said bitterly. "You could at least do me the courtesy of knocking. Or did you wish to catch me unawares to glimpse me naked once more?"

Harlie gave a thin smile, then tossed her hair and strode to where he stood, observing herself in the mirror; a neat frame under a firm, woollen jumper and eyes clearer than glass.

"I'm Honest, Thorne," she said, "not seedy."

He crossed his arms, thick bands of muscle pumping out behind his fists. "Then may I inquire as to your purpose here? The Breathing isn't for two weeks."

Harlie sighed and drew back to the bed, sitting delicately on its edge as if forgetting she'd ever been there before in far less dignified positions. "It's Kayna," she said. "Balvinder claims she is rousing another Evil."

Thorne regarded Harlie from the mirror, without turning. Balvinder claimed many things about Kayna, always concerned with her intrusions on human life. He was Good in all things, and Kayna opposed it with childlike glee. It was a constant battle waged in Ethra, a consequence of Good and Evil living side-by-side over one land.

Thorne was often tempted to turn a blind eye to Kayna's wrongdoings. It was easier that way. However Balvinder had a conscience that couldn't be ignored. He challenged her at every turn, putting an end to her schemes or picking up the pieces when they slipped by him. And where possible, he sought help from the other Essences.

"What type of Evil?" Thorne inquired.

"I'm not certain he knows." Harlie straightened. "But any potent pool of her power must be eradicated. So we have to help him find and destroy it."

Thorne huffed. This was exactly why he avoided the Essences. They were dramatic and nosey and always more than willing to interrupt a good night's sleep and drag him from the comfort of his home. He didn't *need* to sleep, but like eating and talking and walking—he had been granted the privilege. And he quite enjoyed shutting the world out for a few hours at a time. Only that was impossible with acquaintances such as these.

"All right," he said begrudgingly, and retrieved his clothes from the floor. "Though could we not wait for the Breathing? She's never failed to show. Perhaps we could simply ask—"

"No." Harlie's answer came down swift and unassailable. "You cannot *simply ask* anything of Kayna. We should catch her off guard, and let Balvinder lead us to the culmination of her Essence before anything else is to be done. He specifically asked for you."

Gladness roiled in Thorne's bones, barrelling through any sense of his previous reluctance. He was wanted. Needed. "Shall I bring my bow?"

Harlie's eyes glinted. "You'll come then." A statement, more than a question; so Thorne didn't feel obliged to respond. Instead he buttoned his pants, shirt and burgundy waistcoat. Then he strode straight for his armoire and retrieved a long coat with gold trim and a high leather collar, before facing Harlie with a steely expression.

"I don't despise Kayna," he said. "But her power trips are growing tiresome. Must we trail after her for the rest of our immortal existence to clean up her messes?"

Harlie smacked her lips together and rose from the bed. Thorne caught a glint of steel at her hip.

"We're part of a wheel, Thorne. And no matter where our varied opinions lie, Kayna spins with us." Harlie's eyes narrowed in that way that felt like a nail impaling him against a board. "Besides, I get the sense that you rather enjoy her games. That her mess is your opportunity. And that if Balvinder were just as active in his Good works, you'd be similarly inclined to set things wrong."

Thorne grimaced and turned to the door before Harlie could see the smile forming in it. She had painted him as predictably contrary—in a way that nobody else would dare. But she spoke Truth and didn't fear it. He found the notion both maddening and admirable.

"Well," he said, straightening his cloak, "if there's nothing else to interest you in my bedroom, I suggest we make our leave."

Harlie strode to the door and stopped only a few inches away, her eyes unusually bright and unperturbed considering the minimal distance left between them. "I mightn't be opposed. Asha tells me you've spent many years practicing, so perhaps I'll find myself satisfied this time."

Every muscle in Thorne's neck went taut. He had indeed bedded Asha—the Essence of Desire—since Harlie had declined his offer to further their explorations. He had not, however, been aware that this information had been shared.

"What did she say?" he asked, despite himself.

"Mostly positive observations," Harlie mused.

Thorne arched a single, indignant brow. "Mostly?"

Harlie let slip a thin smile. "I can show you the areas in need of improvement, if you'd like."

Thorne straightened, choosing to interpret the comment as an offer. An offer he'd been waiting centuries to refuse.

He drew closer, his lips close to grazing hers.

"You wish," he breathed, and the two words sung sweet, stinging victory.

THREE

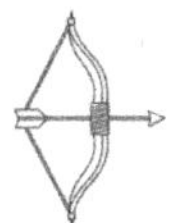

COLT'S OASIS WAS THE MEETING POINT specified by Balvinder. Thorne and Harlie shifted right into it—a swirl of glittering emerald alongside spiralling fuchsia.

As the Essence of Obedience, Colt kept very much to himself unless called upon. Unlike Thorne's home, his was plain and quaint, situated right at the border of the Petrified Forest. It was set down into the dirt, an attempt to remain hidden, though all oases were protected from the human eye. Thorne considered Colt's inconspicuous design a gesture of Obedience to the Overseer, who had instructed the Essences to remain withdrawn from the villages.

Thorne had barely brushed a knuckle upon the front door before it sprung open, and there was Colt—alert and wide-eyed and scrawnier than ever.

"If you spent more time responding to your own needs rather than everybody else's, Colt, maybe you wouldn't appear so malnourished," Thorne said in lieu of a greeting, tapping the boy's shoulder as he strode into the house.

"Welcome Thorne—Harlie." Colt ducked his head and held the door open until they were both well inside. Then he darted to the kitchen table, where he pulled two chairs out from a round table and gestured for them to sit.

Thorne laid his crossbow—an elegant weapon edged in vine-embossed bow irons—and arrow quiver against the chair, before dropping into it.

"I didn't expect you so soon." The mellow voice ran into the room like a smooth current of honey, followed by its source—clad in a pale blue cloak, firm around the torso and sweeping the floor with palpable grace—the Essence of Good stared at them from the doorway.

"Balvinder," Thorne acknowledged, his mouth bending into a smirk. "Don't look so surprised. Punctuality is among many things I Pride myself on."

"Ah, yes." Balvinder moved to the table and took a seat opposite Harlie as Colt rushed to fill the remaining spot. "I suppose the predictability of an Essence dictates a certain reliability of behaviour." His brows—the same silver of his hair, which fell to his shoulders in gentle waves—rose as he considered the thought. "Which is why we're here, after all."

"Might I ask why you felt it necessary to involve Colt?" Thorne inquired, as though the scrawny, sandy-haired boy sitting poised at the other side of the table couldn't hear him.

"Colt was the one who brought this to my attention," Balvinder replied equably. "He encountered Kayna in the forest, and—Colt, you can explain."

The boy seemed to break free from invisible restraints as though he had been awaiting permission, and erupted into his story. "I saw Kayna there, I saw her dragging a body through the Petrified Forest. Not a human body, no. It was a raclor, I think. Yes! A raclor. I do believe it was. Still alive too, before she shifted it away."

"What purpose would Kayna have in snatching a raclor?" Thorne demanded. It can't have been for meat, he thought. Raclors were bony, unpleasant creatures. They were rare too, and he knew of only one area they resided, in deep burrows between Colt and Westby's oases at the border of the forest.

"I have my suspicions," Balvinder mused, sighing heavily. "Shortly after Colt informed me of what he saw, I felt a stirring in the erodosphere. A manifestation of power—Kayna's power. I presume the two events are connected."

Thorne stroked his strong jaw with two fingers. "Did she see you, Colt?"

"I kept hidden," Colt assured him. "She didn't see me, no she didn't."

As Obedience embodied, Colt could be bossed around by the Essences to some degree. They'd all utilised his relentless compulsion to obey over the centuries, but his allegiance was first and foremost with the One who created him. And since the Overseer had laid out a set of rules for the Essences when granting them human forms, Colt was repulsed by those who defied Him.

Thorne could see vexation flickering in those pale, boyish eyes—always unimpressed by behaviour he deemed disruptive to the system.

"Very well," Thorne said finally, and turned once again to Balvinder. "I don't suppose you know where she is?"

Ethra was a vast land—from the humble dwellings of the western continent inhabited by villages like Preo and Emba, to the northern continent and Torena Peaks, the far east Wandrik Isles, and all that fell between—but Kayna had no resting place. She amplified her darkness where she could, and sporadically returned to her oasis, which was buried in the darkest parts of the Petrified Forest.

She had invited Thorne to dine there once, about seventy years ago. Unlike the other Essences, she didn't seem to entirely despise him. At least, she could tolerate him. Though he hadn't stayed long that night. Not only was the place remarkably dreary, but Kayna's agenda proved to extend beyond any civilised sort of desire for company. After serving a dish of meat so rare it practically dripped, she'd attempted to take their *friendship* to greater heights.

Though objectively some might have found Kayna's human form alluring, Thorne couldn't bring himself to bed the Essence of Evil. There was something deeply unappealing in the notion.

And so he had left—which had triggered her tendency toward dark, erotic insinuations whenever they spoke at Breathings, but had also prevented any further dinner invitations.

Balvinder smoothed his hair behind an ear. "I haven't managed to locate her, not yet."

It was an ability of the *Major* Essences, Balvinder and Kayna, for one to be able to sense the path of the other. Their forces were so violently opposed that either presence could be felt from miles away. Similarly, if there was a well of Kayna's Essence, a particularly potent corner of Ethra unnaturally dominated by her—Balvinder could sense it.

Thorne envied that encompassing awareness, amongst other abilities the title of *Major Essence* seemed to afford them. When any of the other Essences dared to speak the word *Minor*, Thorne flamed. For he was complex; perhaps more so than Good or Evil.

Minor Essences were not so confined—they could move from one side of the moral compass to the other, whereas Balvinder and Kayna where stuck at either end.

Thorne had heard Gwin, the embodiment of Optimism, express her contentment over her position many a time. She would often say that being a *Major* Essence involved higher pressure and stakes. That a consciousness in constant battle with an equal opposite would have to be exhausting. Thorne dismissed many of Gwin's arguments, as they were all coated in the same, sickly sweet joy, but he believed she was right about that.

"Well, don't let us delay your search." Thorne waved a swift hand at Balvinder. "And make haste. Best we throttle the snake before it bites again."

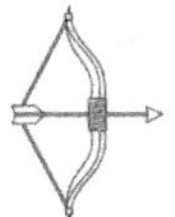

FOUR

THE FOUR ESSENCES SAT IN SILENCE AROUND Colt's kitchen table. Harlie and Colt watched Balvinder intently as he sat as still as stone with his eyes closed. Each lid was so pale and fine that the blue of his gaze could almost be seen through them, darting rapidly left to right. His shoulders dissolved into wisps of blue light, a partial shift from his tangible self into the metaphysical layer baring his truest form.

Thorne impatiently fingered the bristles of arrow fletching jutting out from the quiver resting against his knee.

"Raclors keep to themselves," Harlie muttered, pressing three fingers to her lower lip. "What use would Kayna have with a live one?"

"A pet?" Colt suggested.

"Ah, yes," Thorne drawled. "She likes to keep a few of those."

It was thought that Kayna communicated occasionally with the humans, or rather, a select few. She kept quiet about it, but the Essences suspected that those who had acted out truly horrifically were led by her bidding. And it wasn't just the Essence of Evil accused of such things. Balvinder too had been known to prevent the natural order of life—but his methods weren't so destructive.

Of course neither Kayna nor Balvinder admitted to any such cases, as intercepting the life of any human was forbidden. They seemed to think they were above the rules of the so-called *Minor* Essences.

Thorne shook his head at the thought, and Harlie narrowed those yellow-lime eyes in silent inquiry. He just scowled back.

So she turned to Colt. "Does Nilah know of this?"

"No," Colt answered. "Balvinder doesn't wish to bother her with it."

Nilah Elsternwick … Thorne sighed. Years back, Nilah had been summoned from Earth to dictate the potency of the Essences as the Melder. Though Pacers could hear the voices of the Essences, the Melder was the only human alive capable of *seeing* them. Her task required it.

During Breathings, Nilah's spirit chose what it desired of the Essences, the ratio then magnified and distributed throughout the erodosphere for all spirits to access. She was a bridge between the tangible human dimension and the metaphysical realm.

Thorne often wondered *why* the Overseer felt it necessary to place a mere human at the heart of such a complex system, but he could acknowledge there was some sense in it. It seemed fitting that the free will of all should be allowed through the free will of another—the Overseer's way of re-linquishing control. It was clever, Thorne admitted.

And he enjoyed having at least *one* human able to see him.

Nilah was tolerable company, too. When her chin was lifted high with his Pride, she remained gentle. And though she spoke with authority, there was always an inflection of kindness. Her darkest times had reflected the darkness of the world through war and sickness and slaughter. But still she shone, and Thorne admired her light.

"Nilah is no longer a child," he snapped, impassioned by his train of thought. "Balvinder ought to stop protecting her."

"We will inform Nilah once it's dealt with," said Balvinder, and Thorne cut his gaze to those now-wide blue eyes.

Harlie pressed forward across the table. "Well?"

Balvinder pursed his lips, hesitating a moment. "She isn't far from here—come with me." And with that he rose from the table and made for the front door.

Thorne didn't like to be summoned, so in defiance he sat very still as Harlie and Colt followed Balvinder outside. Colt stopped at the door to shoot him a disapproving glare. But Thorne only smiled. And then, at his own pace, swung his crossbow over a shoulder and seized the quiver as he got to his feet.

The knotted canopy choked out any sight of the midday sun. Green, blue, pink and russet brown momentarily lit the grey trees with vibrant ghosts of colour as the four Essences shifted east within the Petrified Forest.

"We should go the rest of the way on foot," Balvinder declared, straightening the line of his cloak. Thorne grunted his agreement while Colt and Harlie kept silent, moving behind the other two on soft, lithe feet. Neither would offer much help if trouble arose, Thorne considered. Harlie was armed with a dagger, but she was weak. And Colt … he could be simply *told* to leave, and go without so much as a blink of hesitation, if Kayna ordered it. Rather useless really.

They weaved their way through the grim trees without uttering a word. The forest thinned and Thorne's grip on the crossbow tiller tightened as a ghastly fountain came into view. Though many years had passed since he'd come anywhere near this place, he could not forget it; the wide, elaborate base with four stone figures arching from its centre, mangled pain on their straining, cracked faces. A crimson stream seeped out from between them. It flowed steadily down their naked bodies and pooled in the basin below.

There was no doubt in Thorne's mind that it was blood. *Whose* blood, he did not know. And he would not ask. It would be only to indulge an inane curiosity, and seemed a fairly pointless question now, given the victim's current state.

The courtyard featuring the fountain curved up ahead into a single path. Stone trees, rigid with age and dark magic arched over its way, forming a midnight tunnel. Balvinder turned to the others with a wary gaze that commanded instant silence even from their feet, which seemed to soften at his behest, mute against the dirt.

With a flick of his wrist he sparked a flame at his fingertips. It shone a brilliant blue and illuminated either side of the pathway. Thorne slipped his edges into their truest form—hands, feet and chest shifting into luminous green vapour to aid Balvinder's provisional torch.

Another capability Thorne resented—he was able to transform into the light of his Essence, but he could not summon it externally at will like Balvinder. If he could, he would have no need for human mechanisms for burning firewood or lighting his home. He had requested time and time again that the Overseer allow him the ability, but the wish had never been granted. So he stopped asking. He was not the type to grovel.

The path went on further than Thorne remembered. He and Balvinder shed more than enough light for the group. Harlie and Colt followed behind in a darkness that rushed into their wake with a preternatural hunger.

Finally the tunnelled path transitioned into a narrow, stone corridor. It was so seamless that Thorne wasn't entirely sure where the trees had ended and the walls began. But they went on—the stone underfoot ice-cold even through their boots.

Balvinder came to a halt at the corridor's end, looking both ways. His eyes were ghostly blue in the light of the flames still dancing above his long, pale fingers, his skin smooth as marble.

There was an incalculable power radiating from him, as if to be present in the quarters of his natural-born enemy was drawing out his opposing Essence in full force.

With a sharp breath, Balvinder swept right. The others followed suit.

Thorne desperately wished to ask how much further Kayna might be, or if Balvinder knew now what to expect. But it would be foolish to speak when she might be close enough to hear.

So he swept his hair out of his face and kicked his foot into the crossbow stirrup, loading the first arrow with predatory delight.

FIVE

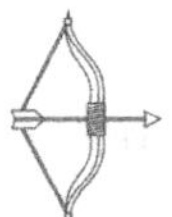

A DIM LIGHT SHONE UP AHEAD—A DOOR AJAR. Balvinder swiftly brought his fingers into a fist and the flame between them melted away.

In a similar vein, Thorne retracted his emerald green tendrils to the shape of his corporeal form as they crossed the remaining distance to the door, waiting then as Balvinder paused for a beat. He was stiff; standing so tall he even marginally exceeded Thorne. Then his eyes shot ahead and he pressed on.

With a hand poised on the bow trigger, Thorne entered a room he immediately recognised. He recalled Kayna's withering gaze across from him at that same sleek, obsidian dining table. A chandelier hung above it, an intricate structure fashioned entirely from fragments of human bone. It would be fascinating if it were not so undignified. Though Thorne supposed it complemented the stench of death permeating every corner of the place.

With long, elegant strides Balvinder turned about the room, watching the walls as though Kayna might be inclined to hide inside them. It wasn't an impossible assumption.

Colt remained stiffly by the door, while Harlie perched on one of the two high-backed chairs, situated at either end of the extensive table.

Thorne couldn't take the silence any more. He went to Balvinder and uttered a hushed, "Where?"

Balvinder considered, and then raised his chin at the next door. But he didn't have to, for at that moment Thorne felt a faint tremor of foreboding. A quiver in the space around them, as though a portion of the realm unseen to most had been disturbed by a dark presence. Spun off-balance.

Without preamble, Thorne whirled toward the next corridor, crossbow raised to his jaw. No injury he could inflict on Kayna would ever be fatal—all Essences were immortal, their bodies a shadow, an elusive representation of what they really embodied. Though, an arrow shot with his strength and precision could slow her down.

Once again as he stalked through the hall, lit by small skylights set into the ceiling that revealed the dull, grey day, Thorne was taken back to that night all those years ago. Kayna had led him this way—to her sleeping quarters— right before she had made her intentions known and he had announced his leaving. She didn't seem at all perturbed by his reluctance, only bemused, and even a little … gratified. As though his apparent repulsion pleased her in some way.

The bedroom was at the corridor's end, he remembered. But the thrum of power didn't seem to stem from there. It was closer. He followed the pull, Balvinder now at his side, sweeping forward like a wolf closing in on its prey.

Balvinder stopped outside a door that stood open enough for black smoke to slip from it and into the corridor. Thorne took no pause; he pushed the door open with his shoulder and swung his crossbow forward.

The room was shrouded in Kayna's foul Essence, though the thin, black-haired female was nowhere to be seen.

Thorne caught movement amongst the shadows. And then he heard it. Rasping breath, the clatter and scraping of chain against stone.

No, Kayna wasn't there. But something else was.

He clutched the crossbow with fierce resolve, striding forward.

Crouched in the corner, its emaciated body heaving with rattling breaths that expelled waves of horrid inky smog—was the raclor.

The raclor raised its angular, disfigured head in a gesture of lolling fatigue. Its claws were tucked close and drawn together. They were longer and sharper than was typical of the creatures. The skin around them was pale, near white, as though life had been drained right out of those leathery fingers. It bore slits for nostrils, as all raclors did, but its eyes were abnormally bulbous and pitch black, devouring all light.

Thorne had always thought Kayna to be rather predictable, but this was new. She was creating a monster; binding her Essence to the creature and forcing herself into its docile spirit.

Charming.

Balvinder took a sharp breath, and as Thorne tightened his grip on the steel crossbow trigger, raised a hand to stop him.

"No," he said—the first word he had uttered since setting foot in the labyrinth of his nemesis.

He sunk to his knees by the raclor, whose enormous eyes fell over him with a mixture of terror and malice. It rose a little at the knees, baring pronged teeth. They were coated in thick blood—its own, Thorne realised.

Raclors were not vicious creatures, nor did they ordinarily have such deadly-looking mouths. This was a twisted, obscene creation. A plaything, or pet—as Colt had suggested earlier.

Balvinder's silvery hair shone white amidst the blackness as he raised a hand out to the trembling creature.

It hissed, those terrible teeth on full display. But Balvinder did not shy away. He reached further, and a silvery web of light slipped out from his fingers. It cut its own path through the black smoke, expanding to enfold the pathetic creature.

The raclor's narrow, pointed ears fell flat against its head, the tips dissolving into black tendrils.

"It has suffered much at her hand," Harlie whispered from Thorne's other side. "This is a darker magic than we've seen yet."

"Yes," Colt agreed, his voice grim as he carefully approached the creature. "Trapping a living, breathing spirit with her Essence. Very troubling indeed. Very troubling …"

Balvinder's calming blue Essence was now dimly reflected in the raclor's wide, bottomless eyes.

"If she has achieved this, perhaps she might—"

"Friends." Colt was cut short by the voice at the door. Thorne felt the word penetrate his bones, like nails tracking the length of his spine.

She stood in the doorway, ebony hair flowing in a sheet to her thighs and lips curled in a half-smile. A black, silk dress encircled her neck, with soaring splits up either side of her body exposing her gaunt frame. She was captivating and horrific all at once.

"I must say, I thought you better than breaching one's private quarters without invitation, Balvinder," she crooned. "It seems unfair to me that I am forbidden from your oases and yet you can walk freely into mine."

"You have disobeyed the Overseer," Colt declared, boldly enough that Thorne found himself vaguely impressed by the little man. "It is forbidden to manipulate the natural order of life forms. *Forbidden*. And you know it."

Kayna angled her head, the movement more than a little animalistic. "What I do in the confines of my home is not for you to dictate."

"And yet it was not in the confines of your home that you found this creature," Balvinder said. The healing strands of his power over the raclor retracted a little, and he took a step toward Kayna. "I will restore his spirit, and then we will release him." His tone was uncompromising—final.

But Kayna's eyes darkened into pits of roiling menace. "You hold no authority here," she hissed. "Step away."

There was a moment of still silence, where even the traces of her Essence permeating the room seemed to slow in their movement.

A rush of shadow spewed suddenly from Kayna's mouth. Her teeth grew suddenly sharp and a web of cracks broke the striking features of her face, exposing darkness beneath.

Thorne fired his arrow a second later and dug his foot into the stirrup to load the next as it struck her chest, where a heart would beat had she possessed one. A shrill cry escaped her and she stumbled.

Balvinder seized the opportunity, lunging out with a flurry of piercing, blue light that swept beneath her feet and knocked her off balance.

Kayna was down only for a moment before she rolled back to standing. Her shoulders shook as she came at Thorne. Grinning. Laughing. The smile enraged him more than her attack—and he raised his bow just in time to release another arrow before she collided into him.

She swung her legs either side of him, two feathered shafts protruding from her torso. With impossible strength, she locked his body against the floor. His crossbow had slipped out of his grip, and his arms were pinned by Kayna's sharp knees.

A flash of steel caught Thorne's eye. Harlie thrashed out with her dagger, but a column of steaming, black tar rose up around them, blocking her attack. Thorne rolled his eyes— he knew she'd be of little help.

Kayna's smile was wild and terrible as she gazed into the face of Pride. "I have often considered such a scenario," she mused. "Though in my imaginings, you were never the one inflicting the pain." She yanked an arrow from her body. Then the other. There was no blood—the wounds healed immediately.

"This was my favourite dress, you know," she said, pouting down at the frayed fabric.

"*Release me*," Thorne barked, snarling like a caged wolf.

The inky column around them pulsed once with blue light, as though they lay at the bottom of the ocean and the sun was forcing its way through the water. Kayna dove forward and brought her lips to his ear.

"Where is the fun in release unless it accompanies the darkest depths of pleasure?" she breathed, the words scraping hungrily down his body.

"I would be interested to hear your definition of pleasure," Thorne said, spitting out a strand of thick hair that had fallen across his face, "for I am far from pleased."

Kayna's murky shield wavered again, and this time the sun exploded through it. She relented a little. Thorne pried out his arm and shoved her off him.

She fell back in a well of shadow, reappearing upright.

Balvinder faced her, palms outstretched as his energy spiralled before him, ready to cast forward. Thorne whipped one of his remaining arrows from the quiver at his back, driving it down into Kayna's nearest bare foot.

Her screech rang out as Balvinder propelled his magic forward. The light swallowed her whole. She thrashed around beneath it, but the luminous trap held its shape. Moments later, she relented. The stillness didn't fall from exhaustion. It was intentional, concentrated. And like a hideous sickness—dark veins began to worm their way from Kayna's centre to the outer shell of Balvinder's snare.

Thorne scrambled for his fallen arrows as another cry came from the corner. He spun to see Colt and Harlie reaching for the raclor, rising now from where it had cowered a moment ago.

There was renewed energy pulsating from its centre, black and callous; any remaining meekness had left it.

Kayna let out a scream, which shattered Balvinder's Essence into jewelled pieces. The raclor broke free of its shackles and roared as they clattered to the floor. It seemed to have grown almost double its original size, towering over them all with talons extended, skin still ghostly white around the fingers, and the rest of its leathery body entirely black.

Kayna's manic laughter rose with the creature, as though every nuance of it propelled the raclor's upward motion, inspiring it to rise too.

"Stop!" Balvinder boomed.

Thorne loaded and fired an arrow at it. The black smoke instantly solidified around the shaft. Thorne was quick. He lurched aside as the arrow was flung back his way and whistled by his ear, grazing the lobe and leaving behind a momentary sting. The cut mended itself in an instant, but sparked a flaming rage in Thorne.

Harlie had turned again on Kayna, her blade gleaming in the light shed by Balvinder's iridescent net drawing towards the raclor.

Both attempts were futile. Kayna disarmed Harlie with a snap of her fingers that commanded a wave of shadow to knock the dagger from her hand, and the beast was rejecting Balvinder's light, its mouth gaping as it devoured the fine blue threads he attempted to project.

Thorne reached for the holster at his hip and brandished his dagger, slashing at the raclor's legs in the same swift movement. Colt came at the creature from behind and wrapped his scrawny arms around its neck. How he possibly thought that was an adequate defense—Thorne had no idea. He huffed a breath of frustration as the raclor flung Colt back against the wall.

With a crack, Colt's head struck stone and he crumpled to the ground.

Nothing is fatal, Thorne reminded himself. And he turned back to the raclor.

It gnashed its needle teeth at him, and before he could act, lunged for his shoulder. Jaws clamped down and Thorne gasped as pain erupted across his torso. Grimacing, he slashed at the beast's head until it reared back roaring and he could pry himself free.

"You have no place here!" Kayna shrieked. "Any of you! Leave us!"

But Balvinder cast his power into a spin. It caught her like a thousand ethereal lassos thrown at once, trapping her arms against her body.

Thorne took a moment to drink in the sight—Kayna held against her will as she'd held him. An involuntary grin broke out across his face.

But then she smiled too.

"Thorne!" Balvinder warned. Too late. Thorne spun back to the raclor and began scrambling for his crossbow— but the beast had sprung past Balvinder and Harlie for the door.

Thorne fired. The arrow pierced the raclor's ear, severing the tip just before it disappeared from view. Good riddance.

Kayna's laughter was shrill. "Quick—after him!" she taunted, not even attempting to break free from Balvinder's restraints. "Run!"

And though he hated following commands—Thorne ran. He raced through the corridor, following the scuttling sounds of the raclor ahead.

He heard the chandelier in the dining room shatter and found himself skidding through the aftermath of broken bones.

The raclor was disappearing through the door to the entrance tunnel, wisps of darkness flaking from its massive body. Thorne paused to load an arrow and then ran, jerking the trigger as he went. It struck the beast square between its sharp shoulder blades. An awful shriek rang out through the tunnel, but the raclor did not slow.

With impossibly even breaths, Thorne sprinted on, his cloak whipping behind him.

It took a great deal of effort to push his human form to the point of exertion. Even when he reached it and felt his throat burning and his chest heaving, he could run on. He supposed every Essence was theoretically granted such endurance, but preferred to think he alone made the most use of it.

The wavering, green outline of his Essence coated his human form like a transparent second skin, illuminating the cave walls. Gritty stone crunched with each pounding step as he followed the raclor from Kayna's lair and along the forest path.

The beast reached the courtyard and crashed to a stop against the stone fountain, dipping its head into the blood and rearing out of it, teeth dripping. Its white claws were also coated crimson, gleaming brilliantly under the few shards of light penetrating the dense canopy.

Another arrow strung—another shot. Right through the creature's leg. Thorne had it now. He was convinced of it. The beast turned its gory head and shrieked, its black eyes hollow and glassy.

"Come on then!" Thorne bellowed. "Fight!" He ditched his crossbow and unsheathed his dagger instead, running straight for the beast.

The raclor launched upward. Thorne slashed and missed. The creature swung up into the canopy as he ducked back for his bow, realising his mistake.

By the time he lifted the weapon, the raclor was making its escape atop the branches.

His shot was obstructed. And the creature would be difficult to chase if he couldn't see its path.

Thorne snarled, his heavy brows knotting fiercely. Outwitted by a mere raclor. He jerked the crossbow further up his shoulder, rage rattling his bones.

Quick footsteps crunched behind him. Colt, wide-eyed and scanning the area, assessing every inch of Thorne.

"Where? Where did it go?" he asked.

Thorne took a great, shuddering breath. "It escaped."

Colt came closer, blinking furiously, as though there was something caught in his eye. "Oh, dear. No."

Pressing his lips into a firm line, Thorne resisted swinging the butt of his bow at Colt's head. "You were no help," he said in the steeliest voice he could muster.

Colt swallowed hard. "It isn't often that I'm required to fight."

"Well, perhaps you ought to learn a few basics," Thorne spat, his breath pumping wildly through his nostrils.

Colt opened his mouth, then closed it. But on second thought, he seemed to summon his courage. "You're a fickle Essence, Thorne, you are," he said. "Your Pride has you resisting assistance, but when things don't go as you expect them to, you blame those whose help you refused. Fickle."

Thorne scowled and turned away. He was well aware that sometimes he contradicted himself—those times his Essence seemed to double up on itself with a differing representation of Pride. He was conscious of attempting to control these little imbalances, and having Colt so blatantly point them out made his blood boil.

When Pride was burned, Thorne did not care to bear the heat alone.

"Go," Thorne barked. "Scurry back to your oasis. *Go on!*"

Colt's hands balled into fists and trembled a little, as though he might've hoped to stay rooted to the spot. But even if he had wanted to, he could not. There were certain direct orders that the Essence of Obedience had no choice but to follow.

Flushed and tight-lipped, Colt rushed past Thorne and into the forest.

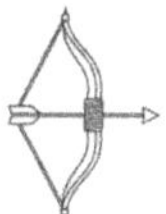

SIX

BALVINDER AND HARLIE FOUND THORNE lazing against the fountain, his arms folded and his face set in hard lines.

"Where is Kayna?" he demanded.

Balvinder's vibrant blue eyes roamed the scene, taking in Thorne and the absence of the raclor. He seemed aware of its escape and—Thorne appreciated—did not point it out.

"She fled," Balvinder said. "We must find the creature."

"Can it shift?" Harlie inquired, curiosity lighting her yellowish eyes.

It was an interesting thought, Thorne conceded. The raclor was so bound to Kayna's Essence that it was almost an extension of her. And *she* was able to transport herself anywhere in Ethra. If this beast were the same, it would certainly wreak widespread havoc.

"Hard to say," Balvinder replied, tapping his chin with one long, slender finger. "Though I doubt it. The creature is possessed by Kayna's power, yes, but it can function only as its physical form allows." He paused, turning over his shoulder to gaze back into that tunnel of darkness.

"We should inform Nilah," Harlie chimed. "She prefers to know of Kayna's meanderings."

"I'll tell her," Thorne declared.

"And I too," Balvinder added, sending Thorne's eyes into a roll that he didn't bother to hide. Balvinder had an odd relationship with the Melder. They were close. Peculiarly close. Granted, they had a complex history, but it was still a little undignified in Thorne's opinion.

"The raclor may have returned to its pack," Harlie commented. "I'll check the border of the forest." She gave Thorne a sharp wink before melting into fuchsia wisps.

Despite an unconventional summoning from Earth to Ethra, Nilah Elsternwick had spread her wings as much as the underground village of Preo would allow. Naivety and wonder were not the only things she brought over from her world—but new life, too. She bore the child far too young, and dealt with the consequences in the midst of deciphering a foreign world of which suddenly, she was at the centre.

Nevertheless, she had always held on tight to her Pride, and Thorne respected that about her.

Every second full moon, Nilah met with the Essences for the Breathings, at which time each Essence offered themself to her spirit. Nilah's choices, her selection of every

Essence, mirrored that of all collective life forms. When her spirit chose a higher portion of Good, it was a reflection of humanity as a whole desiring more of Balvinder's Essence. When she desired Gwin's Optimism, so did others.

And so Nilah restored the balance as the Melder. Over and over again. Her choices did not dictate humanity's choices, nor did humanity dictate hers. Rather, it was a fateful system set in place by the Overseer—whose sight transcended time and conventions. Melders past had, at times, struggled to understand it.

Thorne recalled Nilah's first Breathing. She was so young then; so fragile. But she had stood her ground and accepted the task with such boldness that Thorne could not help but admit himself impressed.

Nilah was now sixty years of age—and despite the faint sketch of time that had begun to show across her skin, she was still beautiful. She had two daughters, Blisse and Zola, both married and with children. And then there was her son Wade, the child born a short while after her arrival in Ethra.

He would have to be close to forty years of age now, and—much to Thorne's distaste—still bore the Insignia of Truth like his mother. Balvinder had helped her raise him as a child, and though Wade couldn't see him, he was well acquainted with the *voice* of Good. Thorne himself had never spoken to the boy.

Reclining against a tree in the Moonlit Woods, Pride watched the sunlight dance across the undergrowth as the pale leaves moved in the wind. Balvinder had shifted into Preo's depths to find Nilah and bring her out from her village.

Thorne didn't often venture below ground level; he felt it both literally and metaphorically beneath him. And the people of Preo happily lived a more primitive lifestyle than he had ever felt comfortable with. So he mostly avoided it.

They appeared a few feet away from him in a sudden, fierce breeze. For a fleeting moment Thorne only saw the girl, held fast by the translucent blue cords that had transported her. And then they sprung back into Balvinder's tall frame, a head of silvery hair catching the light and his piercing eyes appearing inside that pale, marble skin.

"Hello my friend," Nilah said, offering her trademark smile—warm and kind in a way Thorne had seen on no other. She was wearing a long, royal-blue dress that complimented her cascading ash-blonde hair rather nicely, a belt tied around her middle and the Melder's marquise brooch pinned to her chest. Its edges gleamed silver and the polished stone in the centre shone.

Thorne nodded once, allowing an unaccustomed smile to break his hard exterior. "Nilah."

"What is the meaning of an impromptu visit from my two favourite Essences?" she mused.

Thorne rolled his eyes. He knew it was a lie. Nilah had connected most of all with Balvinder, and then with Asha and Harlie. Harlie herself, in all her Honesty, had said as much on multiple occasions.

"Kayna," Thorne said simply, and Nilah's bright, green eyes turned suddenly dark.

"What now?"

Balvinder faced Nilah with a fond look of worry woven into his brow. "She discovered a way to bind her Evil to living things," he said. "We found a raclor at her oasis, possessed by her Essence. I might have been able to save the creature if it hadn't escaped."

Nilah's eyes went wide and Thorne saw a fear in them that made her look twenty years younger. "Escaped?"

Balvinder and Thorne exchanged a glance, a thread of shame mirrored in their expressions. Occasionally they felt similar things, since for Thorne it was possible to dip his toes in either side of morality. These moments of connection were perhaps why Thorne didn't entirely despise Balvinder. They were different, but they could inadvertently share certain nuances.

"The apparitions are trouble enough," Nilah went on with a shudder. "I daresay I would pay you all more visits if they didn't lurk between us."

Thorne huffed his agreement. The apparitions were ghastly creatures. A mirror image of their victim—but with black eyes, elongated limbs and ferocious teeth. Kayna, knowing her magic could not breach the oases of the other Essences, had set them in place around the Petrified Forest, to taunt and make a nuisance of themselves. Thorne guessed the Overseer allowed it as a way to ensure the humans steered clear.

"And this is far worse," Balvinder said. "Kayna conjures the apparitions from nothing but her own dark magic and those they reflect—but the raclor was an innocent life form, imprisoned against its will."

A flash of uncharacteristic rage crossed Nilah's face. Her nostrils flared as she breathed deeply and seemed to consciously repress the rush of anger. "Well then," she said, "I see only one solution."

Balvinder and Thorne looked to each other again, awaiting more.

"Kayna has too often disregarded the boundaries set for us," Nilah continued, the smoothness between her brows unusually disturbed. "She must be contained. Locked away. Confined between Breathings."

Thorne's stone hard expression transformed into one of triumph. But when he returned his gaze to Balvinder, he saw something quite unexpected. Reservation.

Though what else was to be expected of the Essence of Good, he thought with no small amount of long-suffering agitation.

"I do agree," Thorne conceded, attempting to override the doubtful glint in Balvinder's eyes. "She has no right to freedom, not when she weaves paths of destruction all over Ethra and leaves us to pick up the pieces."

But Nilah was only looking at Balvinder, searching his face for an answer to the evident hesitation in it.

"Whatever we make of Kayna," Balvinder finally said, his voice soft, "She does allow for choice, you see. She attends Breathings willingly, and offers herself to human spirits, so they might take from her Essence."

"Our worlds would be far better off without her," Thorne stated gruffly, folding his arms and angling his head so that the other two could only be seen by looking down his nose.

Balvinder shook his head. "Once, there was the world that you speak of. The Overseer created Earth first, a land void of Essences and spirits. The erodosphere did not exist, only the shells of humans to roam and feed and breed. But, you know what became of it …"

Thorne pressed his lips firmly together. He did not respond well to Balvinder's history lessons. He knew it all back to front, better than anybody else. He did not need—

"Nothing," Balvinder said. "He had created a land without a people who were capable of appreciation—of Pride, Thorne." Thorne's irritation wavered at that, and he allowed himself to enjoy the sentiment, though he knew Balvinder likely only said it to soften him. "Of loving and hating and understanding," he went on. "So He fashioned Ethra, and there the metaphysical could exist and conjoin with Earth, sustaining a dual dimension that allowed for a human spirit. For freedom of choice. Our bodies are recompense for our captivity of emotion. To confine Kayna now would defy the equality of freedom gifted to us as Essences."

"How very touching," Thorne retorted, flashing a plastic smile that was gone almost as soon as it appeared. "But Kayna deserves no gifts. She does not understand or appreciate the privilege of freedom. She can't—"

"Thorne's right," Nilah interjected, leaving him unsure whether to feel appalled at the interruption or pleased by her agreement. "You speak as if she's just like the rest of you, Balvinder, but she isn't and never will be. Time and time again it has been proven." Nilah shifted on her feet and cast a rapid glance around the woods, as if fearful Kayna might emerge from a shadow between the trees. "Thorne is right."

She had said it twice, now. "Say it again," Thorne crooned, a smirk tugging at his lips.

"Oh dear me, no," Nilah replied. "Your head might explode."

Unimpressed, Thorne strode away and pressed his arm against a nearby tree. He knew Nilah to be easily swayed by Balvinder's opinion, and therefore there was nothing left to do but await it.

At last, Balvinder spoke. "If you order it, Nilah, we will see it done," he said. "If the Overseer deems it a violation of the rules, He will make that known."

Only Thorne—after a friendship with Balvinder spanning thousands of years—could detect the lingering reluctance in his tone.

Nilah however, nodded gravely. "I suspect it won't be a simple task."

"Simple is boring," Thorne said, strolling back to rejoin them. "Kayna has had her fun. Now it's time for us to have ours."

He remembered the hard stone floor beneath him as she had straddled his waist, unrelenting. He felt her inky black hair catch in his mouth. The shadows swarming him. Her cold, callous laughter. "Tonight," he said, gasping a little from the rage caught in his throat. "We catch that bitch tonight."

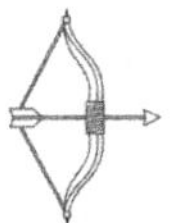

SEVEN

RAIN SHOT IRIDESCENT, GOLD DROPLETS OVER the small travelling party, swamping the fields before them and soaking through their clothing.

Thorne was far from pleased.

"Could we not have shifted any closer?" he inquired tetchily.

Behind him, Nilah was clutching Balvinder's arm for balance. Thorne wondered what her blaze—Myron—would think of the gesture. According to him, the Breathing days were simply time she spent up in the woods to meditate. He did not know of Nilah's role as the Melder, and in turn knew nothing of her friendship with Balvinder.

Friendship. If that was in fact what it was.

"We mustn't alert Kayna to our presence," Balvinder said. His silver hair glittered in the golden rain, plastered to every delicate angle of his face like streaks of liquid stardust.

Nilah nodded and agreed, "Better to catch her unawares. Then we can try speaking reason into her."

Tightly pursing his lips, Thorne decided it wasn't worth his time to challenge the notion. But really, it was rarely possible to *reason* with Kayna. It was as if Nilah hoped to persuade her into shackles. Have her see the logic in the decision to seize her freedom. The idea was so absurd that Thorne could barely withhold his snigger.

Nilah had a nasty habit of wishful thinking, something she must have picked up from that pesky little Essence of Optimism—Gwin.

He wondered what the rosy-cheeked girl might be up to. Blissfully unaware of all this commotion, no doubt. Crafting flower crowns and capering about Maravier perhaps. She spent much of her time there—the garden province. Thorne suspected she had some input in Maravier's impressive, lush estates and thriving floral designs. The Pacer of Maravier accepted quite a significant amount of Optimism, and he was sure Gwin had used this to connect with her, as Thorne had done with Pacer Barlon of Rylora.

"How will you restrain her?" Nilah asked Balvinder as they followed behind in the slush.

"In any ordinary situation, Kayna and I are fairly evenly matched," Balvinder said. "But if I choose to, and if I strike first, I can hold her in place."

Mud sucked at Thorne's boots, gold specks swirling paths through it like oil running over water. With each step he winced. He had acquired the shoes at an upmarket store in Rylora. Left money on the counter, of course. They would have been easy to steal, but Thorne adhered to a certain standard of honour, and thievery did not feature. Granted the money itself he *had* taken from Thanron's mints, where all coins were cast.

He scowled as his shoes sunk deeper into the mud. Balvinder had insisted they shift to the outskirts of Tarling, a town in the River Knot. This was where he claimed to sense Kayna's presence. They weren't far from the southern jungles of Tithonelia, where she was known to meddle with witch-ridden tribes.

Pitched rooftops and rows of clustered wooden houses drew faint lines through the pelting rain.

Finally, Thorne thought bitterly.

Tarling was relatively desolate due to the weather. Most of the townspeople were clever enough to remain inside or undercover, and aromas of roast meat and smoke from their chimneys filtered through the air.

Essences didn't hunger or thirst. They were capable of eating and drinking nothing at all, in fact. Their bodies would remain regardless of whether they were sustained or not. Each had been crafted by the Overseer, immortal and somewhat tangible. But despite this, the scent of a hot meal teased Thorne's taste buds as it would anyone else's.

"Where to now?" he inquired without bothering to veil his rising impatience.

Balvinder scanned the rain-shrouded town. "This way," he said. And they walked on, this time with Balvinder in the lead.

A few townsfolk bent curious glances their way. To the common eye, it was only Nilah braving the rain—an unfamiliar woman with sodden hair dripping miserably past her waist, walking by their homes without any defined sense of direction. She would be sure to arouse suspicion.

"Walk with purpose," Thorne hissed. "When you raise your chin, you deflect doubt. Including your own."

Nilah was astute enough to say nothing, but her mouth curved in a gentle smile and she lifted her chin a little.

Balvinder turned swiftly. His blue gaze was honed and intent, and he nodded once—then dived into a narrow space between two shop fronts.

Unlike the others, Thorne was required to turn sideways to fit his crossbow and massive shoulders through the gap, but to his relief slate roofs covered the avenue and the ground was dry. He dragged a hand through his wet hair and cast a dubious eye over Balvinder, who had stopped with his back to one wall and his hand flat against the other.

Thorne opened his mouth to demand a progress report—when Balvinder's head snapped right. He strode the rest of the way along the avenue without a word. Nilah hurried after him. With a gruff sigh of resignation, Thorne dug his foot into the stirrup of his crossbow to prepare an arrow, and then followed.

When he rounded the corner Balvinder was stalking toward the river, now visible between clusters of houses supported by timber stakes ahead. Ramshackle walkways made slippery by the rain led to each door, but Balvinder was making for one in particular.

"Nilah, you stay here," he said. Thorne nodded his assent, elbowing past her. If they were to speak to Kayna without any villager picking up on the disturbance, it wouldn't help to have Nilah barging through in all her blatantly human visibility.

Reluctantly, she agreed.

Balvinder shifted inside and Thorne hastily followed suit, keeping his bow raised to his chin even as he wafted from his emerald-green form and back to his body at the opposite side of the door.

Upon a rapid scan of the room, he noted plants dried and strung across the ceiling in a messy tapestry, shelves cluttered with glass jars containing worms and insects and lizard-like creatures suspended in yellow liquid, and two humans at a low table—one a young woman and the other a bald, middle-aged man in grey robes. He clutched her arm. Blood dripped down the sides of her slender wrist and into a stone dish. Around them, darkness bloomed and whispered in shuddering streaks and bursts, tendrils slipping into the man's open mouth.

"It is here," he was saying, his eyes black as night. "It hears us."

Thorne's nostrils curled at the putrid stench of death and decay polluting the air. The dark cloud seemed to falter, freeze momentarily—and Balvinder seized the hesitation.

He thrust out his arms and streams of power surged from his entire body, enveloping the darkness and the humans inside it.

A rancorous shriek rattled the shanty so violently that even the young girl cast a look of terror about the room.

The cords of Kayna's Essence lashed at Balvinder's. Her black tongues spat venom and the man touched by her Evil slumped in his chair, dropping the girl's bloodied arm into the dish.

"Matcham!" she cried, seizing his quivering hands.

Thorne held fast to his crossbow. He could only slow Kayna with the weapon if she chose to appear in her physical form.

The girl stared at Matcham intently as colour slipped back into his eyes. Neither were aware of what was taking place around them in the eternally invisible layer of the Essences, and never would they be.

Despite everything, Thorne couldn't dissuade the smirk that appeared at the thought of their naivety. Clearly this man fancied himself a sorcerer of sorts, and the girl had sought him out for it. They were playing a dangerous game— one that no amount of spells or summoning or pickled innards would ever bring to light.

Gradually the malicious smog clung to a frame bound in tight, blue webs, and that frame became Kayna, baring her teeth and staring out at them with bulging eyes blacker than the darkest depths of the sea. She wore a thick, hooded cloak and her skin was as pale as bone under its shadow.

"What is the meaning of this?" she hissed. The rage seething beneath her tone fell away a little as an impish smile turned her mouth. "Did you crave my company so drastically that you could not wait until the Breathing to see me?"

Balvinder allowed himself a smile, but it was tight and unnatural. "There are matters we must discuss," he said. "And now there is one more." He kept his hands out toward her to maintain the firm restraints, but his eyes shifted to the humans.

"Matcham, *please.*" The girl's voice broke, tears spilling from her pale brown eyes. "What does it say? *Tell me.*"

"I am not an *it*, little girl," Kayna drawled, casting a weary eye back at her. "These humans never learn, do they?" She directed the question at Thorne, who might've been inclined to agree had she not caused him so much grief in the past couple of days.

He returned his arrow to the quiver and swung the crossbow over his shoulder, unsheathing his dagger instead. This would now become, he imagined, a close-range interrogation.

"Who is she?" Balvinder demanded. "The girl—what purpose does she have with a sorcerer?"

Kayna's lips parted into a full, wolfish grin. "Her mother is dead, if you must know, and now her father is ill. She is in search of a power to heal him, and Matcham Cleaver here summoned me by her blood. Would you refuse such a delicious invitation if it were delivered to you on a platter?"

"I don't recall healing the sick as your specialty," said Thorne, approaching her with a smug flourish of his dagger.

Kayna's thin, black brows arched high. "I am capable of much."

"It isn't healing if you mend wounds only to leave un-invited parts of yourself beneath them," Balvinder said, his voice hard.

Kayna had a habit of instilling greater portions of her Evil between the beats of a suffering human heart before making it whole again. The sense of entitlement was repulsive. Though Thorne knew that if he was capable of offering more of himself to those who lacked his Essence, he might be tempted to do the same.

"Matcham," the girl sobbed. "*Answer me.*"

Balvinder's face furrowed at the sight of her sorrow, as though it linked irrevocably with his own deep-rooted empathy, characteristic only of the purest Good. The luminous net around Kayna contracted so fiercely she released a guttural growl.

The bald sorcerer—Matcham Cleaver as she called him—finally drew back to himself, blinking like a madman.

"It's ..." he hesitated. "Gone."

Kayna rolled her eyes. "Fool."

"Actually," Thorne said, driving his dagger forward until the point dug into the taut flesh of Kayna's neck, "he's right—you're leaving."

Balvinder, after a mournful glance at the young girl whose wrist still seeped blood, drew his fingers together and swept Kayna into a netted cocoon of luminous blue. Then he shifted out of the room, taking her with him.

Thorne looked once more at the young girl and Matcham the sorcerer.

"Will it help my father?" she asked, eyes wide and earnest.

Matcham hesitated with a finger to his lips. "For twenty copper greats, I am sure it will do its utmost."

Anger coursed through every nerve in Thorne's body. The sorcerer was exploiting the girl, making a joke of the Essences and the unseen.

She looked uncertain, but then reached for her pocket and retrieved a small, leather satchel. Thorne couldn't stand by and watch the transaction.

He grabbed the edge of the table and in one swift movement—flipped it on its head.

Matcham leapt to his feet and the girl fell right out of her chair as the bowl of her blood broke across the slate floor. In a panic, she turned and fled.

Thorne grinned and strolled out the door after her, peering back at Matcham, who looked satisfactorily baffled.

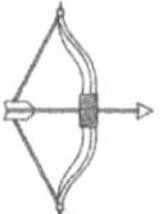

EIGHT

THE GROUP FIRST SHIFTED KAYNA TO THE outskirts of Tarling. The sky was clear, and a dew of golden rain tipped every blade of grass and patch of dirt. Balvinder kept his fingers clutched and Kayna trapped in the grip of his extended Essence. Nilah's mouth was set in a hard line, her eyes locked on his cage.

"Would you kindly explain the meaning of this, dearest Melder?" Kayna inquired, tossing her hood back away from her face. Every angle of it was striking—hard, slanted cheekbones below a broad forehead and vast, black eyes.

"Enough is enough," Nilah declared. She lifted her chin higher, and a shiver of Pride coursed through Thorne's body. "We are taking you away for safekeeping. And by that, I mean the safety of others."

Kayna lifted a brow. "You mean to detain me?"

"Don't pretend you haven't brought this upon your own head," Thorne snapped. "Freedom is a right you've well and truly lost."

Balvinder's blue web wavered, and Thorne cut a glance at his expression—set and unrelenting, but overlaid by … doubt? Pity?

"*Balvinder*," Thorne warned—and the fluid cage stiffened again. One slip and Kayna would break free from the restraints. This was no time for doubt or pity. They needed to take her somewhere contained.

"All Essences are granted bodies," Kayna said through her teeth. "*All.*"

"But not *all* Essences leave a path of destruction in their wake," Nilah pointed out. Her chin was still tilted high and her hair had dried after the rain into soft, ashen waves. Thorne took a moment to admire the Melder in full—so fierce and so gentle all at once. "You have been given chance after chance, Kayna. Having you roam free is too great a risk."

"And you consider this fair, Balvinder?" Kayna spat.

Thorne's unease grew as Balvinder's lips thinned.

At last, he spoke. "If He hasn't intervened yet, perhaps the Overseer Himself wills it."

Kayna drew back her head and cackled into the grey sky. And then—so suddenly that not even Thorne saw it coming—she lurched forward and collided with him.

His torso turned to glistening emerald ribbons and a dark tendril of Kayna's power clutched at them. He roared at the searing pain channelled through the touch. In a writhing frenzy he shifted the rest of his body into the erodosphere and back again, attempting to free himself. Again. And again. But her grip had turned to an inky tar, forcing him closer in every dimension.

Balvinder's Essence pulled across her shadowy clutches to assist Thorne's escape—and that minute distraction was all it took. Shadows burst free from the opposite side of the net. Kayna spun out like a tornado at the heart of a storm, rapidly casting a wall of pitch darkness to shield herself.

Thorne slunk back to his body, stumbling off balance. It was Nilah that steadied him, though he quickly brushed her off.

Balvinder whirled and slammed his hands against Kayna's shield. Scorching, blue veins crept across the glass, but didn't breach further. He pressed forward and released a cool breath of air. The black glass turned frosted, transparent enough to display Kayna standing deathly still behind it. Shadows spun from her fingertips and bloomed like a poisonous flower at her back.

"And to think a mere human convinced you to defy the ancient sanctions of the Essences." Kayna clicked her tongue, and then ran it across her lips as she smiled. "I'm devastatingly disappointed."

"Human, yes," Nilah conceded. "But I am also the Melder, and the Overseer set me in place to act as your authority."

Thorne didn't like the sound of that, but he only frowned and kept his mouth shut.

"We will hunt you down if we have to, Kayna. Too much damage has been done—" Nilah's voice cracked on the final word. Thorne glanced at her—at the fresh tears running smoothly down her cheeks. He urged her to go on. It would do no good to demonstrate any weakness in this moment. "And you," Nilah recovered, "your reign has ended."

Kayna inclined her head, the ghost of a smile crossing her lips. "Oh, dear Nilah," she muttered. "I am beginning to think you are under the grave misconception that if I cannot kill you, you remain immune to me."

Thorne knew that Kayna despised the magic protecting Nilah from any permanent damage. No Essence could kill or inflict permanent harm on the Melder, and vice versa. But now, there was a delighted glint in Kayna's eye. The flicker of a revelation that chilled Thorne's core without his permission.

Nilah seemed to notice it too, for she took a reactive step back.

"You are an easier target than you realise," hissed Kayna. "For you are one, but you are many."

And with that—she vanished.

Nilah was in a state of distress. Even she had pieced together the meaning of Kayna's departing words.

"My family," she breathed, grasping the crook of Balvinder's arm. "She'll go after them—do terrible things Balvinder, *terrible* things."

"Taking her freedom is unforgivable in her mind," Thorne commented. "Which is *why* we were supposed to succeed the first time." He shot an accusatory look Balvinder's way. But he didn't see it. He was staring at Nilah, his blue gaze alert.

"Where are they?" he asked. "Myron? Blisse and Zola? The children?"

Nilah's eyes darted left to right, as if they stood before her to be counted. "All in Preo, though …" She pressed a finger to her lips until they lost colour. "Blisse. She and Ansel planned to take Zacharias into the woods tonight. To sleep under the stars."

Zacharias. Nilah's ten year-old grandson—Thorne recalled. There were oh so many names, and he cared very little for the Melder's irrelevant extended family, all bustling around under that ant hive they called Preo.

Balvinder breathed deeply and closed his eyes. "Allow me a moment to gauge her direction."

Thorne folded his arms and his heavy brow furrowed deeply. He had the sense that this was bound to end horribly. Anything involving Kayna often did. And an angry, rogue Kayna could be even worse.

Nilah fixed her attention on Balvinder and seemed to cease breathing for the span of his silence.

Then his eyes flashed open. They were a darker, churning blue to their usual electric shade. His expression was like immovable stone.

"Preo," he whispered. "She is moving for it. And fast."

NINE

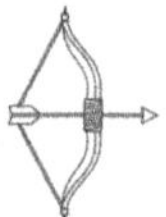

ETHRA'S VAST SUN WAS SETTING OVER THE
undulating houses of Emba, casting shadow waves across
the dirt and cobblestone paths.

After a swift detour to Kayna's oasis, Thorne shifted
into the village square holding a bag that now clanged
against his hip. It held the shackles Kayna had used to
confine the now deranged raclor. He smiled to himself. It
would be a nice addition to her cell.

A young tree grew from the centre of the square.
Villagers passed by it without a glance in Thorne's direction. They carried sacks, babies, cartons or trays of produce.

It was a tragedy that most humans were unable to see
the Essences, or even so much as know of their existence,
Thorne thought with a sombre sigh as he gazed around
at their faces. And he was not the only one to consider
it unfair. Peirce—the Essence of Pessimism—was useful
for when Thorne wished to discuss the injustice of it all.
Mostly he was an outright bore and a perpetual wet blan-
ket, but he had his sporadic redeeming moments.

Thorne stopped by the wheat fields amidst the remaining farmers finishing their day's work. He drank in the sight of the gilded crops spread beneath the sinking sun and considered how spectacular he must look in harmony with the picturesque landscape. Ebony. Ivory. Gold.

Emba was known for its proficient cultivation. Westby—the Essence of Efficiency—had taken it on as his pet project long ago, along with an underground water system. He had left seeds of the idea with Pacer Aubrin, the leader of Emba.

Many of the Essences were known to drop the odd intervention here or there. Like Gwin, with her contribution to the gardens of Maravier. Or his own assistance in Rylora's design. But none of these instances resulted in disaster, like they did with Kayna.

Thorne raked a hand through his hair and drew in a deep breath. No wonder the Overseer restricted the Essences to eternal isolation. Kayna's reputation tainted them all, and Thorne hated her for it.

With renewed vengeance simmering under his skin, Thorne melted into glistening green vapour and cast himself through the dark dimension to settle before a grand, stone house situated a few yards away from a river.

Framing the front door were two tall pillars of wood aged to stone, boasting whorls of grey, silver and black. It was a house constructed by the Essences long ago for Melders past to hold gatherings, built from trees procured from the Petrified Forest. They had once often utilised it when Raphe—a previous Melder hundreds of years back— had made Emba his primary home between Breathings.

Now, with Nilah living in Preo, it was relatively abandoned. And a brilliant hiding place, as most villagers avoided it at all costs. They believed the forest to be haunted, cursed, and a similar reputation hung about the house.

Thorne grinned as he shifted beyond the doorway and into the main, dark corridor. The theories and superstitions held by the humans never failed to amuse him. They fabricated the most elaborate of fancies, and believed utter lies with all of their tragic, little hearts. None here knew the Truth, aside from Pacers of course.

In Emba, the Pacers had always chosen to hide their Truth Insignias. Thorne supposed the people were already so superstitious, their leaders hoped to avoid further whispered conspiracies.

Though in Preo, the underground hive Nilah called home, a formal ritual had developed. There they upheld the Insignia as a symbol of Truth granted by an unseen entity, and made a fuss over the process. It was handled differently across all of the four main continents in Ethra, the Overseer allowing each body of people to react as they chose, but *all* Pacers knew of the unseen world.

At least there was a little recognition from those who held authority. Those that mattered. On Earth, most were entirely ignorant.

Thorne scowled at the thought while turning his hands to luminous green tendrils, lighting his way along the black corridor.

There were nine rooms, four either side of the corridor and one at its end. Most were set up as sleeping quarters on the off chance that the Essences wished to stay there instead of returning to their oases. One—Thorne thought with grim pleasure—would soon become Kayna's prison.

He scouted out the place, turning his nose at the general coating of dust and cobwebs adorning every crevice and furnishing. Rather fitting for the Essence of Evil, he decided. It would do very well.

He emptied a room of its small bed and table, and then reached into the bag he had brought containing the shackles Kayna had used on the raclor. He hammered them into the stone with nails the size of his fingers.

With each strike he tasted sweet victory, for all the grief that witch had caused him and others. This was centuries overdue.

Thorne straightened and swept back the locks of hair that had fallen loose.

Balvinder would find a way to seal his magic to the shackles while draining Kayna's to ensure escape was impossible. But even then, Thorne suspected they would be required to strengthen the prison as time went on and her rage only grew.

And then there were the Breathings. They may be permitted to lock Kayna away, but not to restrict her contribution to the erodosphere altogether. So long as spirits desired her Evil, she would offer it to them, and none of the Essences could obstruct *that*. It was the process of free will, after all.

They would need to be certain Kayna would have no possible means of escape when they shifted her to each Breathing. It wouldn't be easy. Though, it was better than allowing her free reign between times.

After checking the room for cracks in the walls and floor, Thorne considered his work done. The rest was up to Balvinder.

He wondered how he was faring against Kayna in the Moonlit Woods—and if she had got far with wreaking revenge on Nilah by terrorising her family. It was a clever move, Thorne had to admit.

A distant cry whispered through the stone. It was faint, and yet the terror alive in its tone had Thorne snapping to attention. Not the exclamation of a child—but a woman.

He wafted into vapour and reformed near Emba's heart on a dirt pathway between rows of close-knit homes.

Another scream. And then a wail that would have curdled his blood had any run through his veins.

He had left his crossbow at his oasis before inspecting Kayna's cell—he had only his dagger. But it ought to be enough. Threats in Emba were likely restricted to night insects or strong winds, or at the worst of times—stray wolves.

He stalked between the houses and there was a shout, loud and panicked and this time from a man. Thorne's brow narrowed and he quickened his pace, reaching for his dagger.

The path veered suddenly into a corner of the village square. He stopped in his tracks and took in the sight before him; frenzied villagers, some wailing and others rushing forward to the central tree in the square, more bursting in from side streets. His gaze fell upon the array of dark shapes heaped around the base of the tree.

Moonlight caught the planes of a smooth complexion, wan and frozen. Thorne stiffened. A youth. Perhaps no older than thirteen.

He passed by the frantic villagers and caught broken glimpses of the other victims. All children. All drained of their spirit.

Another wilting scream tore through the night. Shadows bloomed around the tree's branches and obscured Thorne's view but as they parted, the stack of victims slumped under the weight of two new bodies.

The shadows whipped away and into a far side street. Thorne didn't waste a second. He surged ahead, bending into brilliant green light as he went.

Stray strands of blackness joined Kayna's rocketing form, as though thrilled to have found its most potent source. She cut left. Thorne followed the trail of her fetid scent—right to the door of a small, round-roofed home.

Kayna seeped around the wooden frame. Thorne hung back only for a second. There was a chance she hadn't noticed he was after her. If she realised too soon, he could lose his edge.

The cries of the villagers were distant from here; they had covered a mile or so in a few seconds. Thorne snapped his focus to the sky, an idea dawning on him.

With elegant ease, he leapt into the air and slipped into his Essence, continuing up, up, up to the shingle roof. He landed softly and in the same movement, melted through the slates.

He looked down upon a bedroom—where a couple rested soundly in each other's arms. Not there. He drew back above the roof and repositioned himself.

This time, he sunk into a room with walls decorated in garish paint; green hills brushed with carefree strokes, figures drawn in haphazard lines, and all sorts of wild creatures that only a child would imagine into life.

A young girl was asleep in her bed—presumably the hand behind the art. Beside her, as thick and lethal as the deadliest of nights, a feminine form rose from between the timber floorboards. The ghostly dark looked upon the girl, failing to see Thorne hovering above.

Time seemed to slow as Kayna reached down through skin and bone, seizing the pulsing spirit of the little girl between her taloned fingers.

TEN

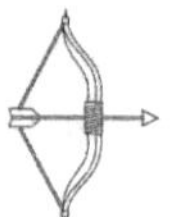

THORNE SLIPPED DOWN LIKE LIQUID JADE, spreading his Essence into a lattice-like net. He let hair-thin tendrils form at every edge of him, all working to hook themselves into Kayna's translucent body. A choked shriek rang out as the green cords looped around her neck, yanking tight.

Kayna had released her grip on the girl's spirit, writhing in a mess of shadow and malice. He had caught her at the right time, poised between Essence and body.

It would be impossible to keep her long, but he contracted fiercely nevertheless, willing the strength he needed.

The girl sat upright, glancing about the room as fear wrung her small mouth into a twist. Her hair was rumpled and her eyes a dull green.

She senses us, Thorne realised. In touching her spirit and not yet destroying it, Kayna had alerted the girl to their presence.

A glow emanated from her nightgown, glistening white gold—the centre of her choices, of her freedom. Her spirit. And Kayna was prepared to tear it away.

"Leave her," Thorne hissed, his net straining against the dark. "You've done enough."

"Oh, my beauty," Kayna whispered, the inky-black turning bone-white as edges of her face illuminated. "It's never enough."

"Hello?" The little girl's murmur filled the space around them.

Kayna's lips curled at the sound of it, still broken by wisps of shadow. Her head circled around to peer down at the girl, dark smoke drawing the twisted lines of her neck. "It would be rude not to answer."

"Stop it," snapped Thorne. He revealed his face an inch from hers and spat his words into it. "Why do all this? Children—they're only *children*."

"How very astute," Kayna answered, flashing her grey teeth in a smile that cut through her cheeks.

The little girl slipped back under her covers and pulled them right over her ears. Her eyes were still wide open though, peeping over the duvet.

Thorne cut his attention back to Kayna. "You're angry we proposed your imprisonment," he said. "But surely you can see that this is *not* the way to convince us otherwise."

Kayna rocked her head closer and let out a rasping, guttural laugh. "You still seem to think I care what you make of me, that I am held to some higher standard you all adhere to and I should be foolish enough to uphold too."

"You can't be trusted."

A frown touched Kayna's wide brow. "An obvious observation, I would have thought."

Thorne scowled and squeezed her harder. "With freedom comes power. If you plan on pursuing the latter, you can't run about destroying everything in your path."

Kayna only inclined her head as if to contemplate the sentiment. "I appreciate your appeal to my hunger for power, though it's almost as transparent as you are right now."

In a flash of rage, Thorne fabricated his right hand and struck out. His dagger cleaved through what parts of Kayna's flesh it could catch in her semi-lucid state. Though it was enough to make her flinch.

He seized his opportunity and heaved her across the room, rippling through a half-moon window. They hung a few feet off the ground, Kayna suspended in his clutches— which he hated to admit were rapidly weakening.

"You were headed for Preo," he muttered. "Balvinder said—" and then he stopped. Of course Kayna had fooled them somehow, and it would do him no good to point out that they had fallen right into her deception.

"I left a gift there for the Melder," whispered Kayna. "I am sure they will find it soon enough."

Thorne dreaded to think what she meant by that. He also wondered what *was* in fact taking Balvinder so long. Kayna executing a series of acts so horrible was bound to alert him. He usually sensed imbalances in the erodosphere. So where was he?

As Thorne debated whether he was strong enough to drag her to the prison himself, shadows began to collect behind her shoulders. "If my fun is over, at least let me enjoy the aftermath," she said, as the dark drew from stray strands of her Essence to form two reflections. Both swam with the deadly grace of Kayna herself, female outlines wavering around triangular smiles and gaping sockets for eyes.

Thorne cursed as another two appeared. And then all four lunged at him.

They screeched and slashed, breaking through the network of his strands holding Kayna. Though made of shadow, their claws shredded him apart. Pain seared through every particle of his being until he hung in ribbons.

Kayna burst into laughter and her shadow reflections unleashed beastly echoes of the sound. Wisps of hair like smoke poured from their heads and danced gleefully around them.

With an effort, Thorne stitched himself back together. And by the time he had just managed to form fingers, and a face, and a chest—the shadow women rushed at him.

All his attempts to resist were futile. The erodosphere whirled in coloured flecks and streams around him until the world cleared, and the square came back into view.

He was shoved to the lowest rooftop. Before he could gather his wits, Kayna was behind him with the steel of his own dagger held cold against his neck. The sensation drew his entire human form out from hiding. Kayna's was too—he could feel her hard body against his back.

Below them, the crowd of villagers had doubled. Most were unravelling; on their knees, sobbing, holding each other, aimlessly scouring the area for a perpetrator they would never find. It was denial and chaos and tragedy—and Kayna fed on it, as though watching the impact of her Evil renewed it in some vital way.

The shadow women from earlier had swept down to dance and cackle above the centre tree, under which the children lay.

But, through the blackness, which permeated most of the square, tendrils of electric blue shone out. The villagers were breathing a chaotic mix of the two. The murders were Evil, but the grief they felt—that was a shade of Good. An opposing force. Balvinder was there, at least in that.

"You know he will have your head for this," Thorne said coarsely, gritting his teeth as the blade pierced his skin.

"Will he?" Kayna murmured thoughtfully. "I'd say the worst Balvinder might do is lock me away—though ... that was already his plan, was it not?"

Thorne snarled and attempted to shift into his Essence. But she had him in her clutches somehow, making it impossible. "You're disgusting."

Kayna's tongue flicked against her teeth. "You certainly know how to flatter a lady."

"It wasn't a—"

The sky exploded.

Bursting through the night, casting aside streams of inky dark, a sapphire light erupted over the square.

Thorne was knocked off his feet by the force of it. He cushioned the fall by shifting into his Essence before he struck the ground. Maniacal laughter burst from Kayna's gaping mouth as she stood with her arms outstretched, as if in welcome.

Surging forward, Thorne struck at her wrist and dived for the dagger as it clattered to the slate roof. Then he straightened and watched as cerulean blue flame dissolved the dancing shadow reflections in the square to ashy flakes.

Balvinder swarmed over Kayna, stifling the sound of her laughter.

A pervasive sorrow flooded the square. An ache so powerful that Thorne himself shuddered from its throbbing shock.

Hundreds of silvery hands moulded Kayna's meandering shadows, compressing her into one tangible, slender body.

No chinks of doubt showed in Balvinder's attack. No sympathy. His purpose was clear and singular.

"The house is ready," Thorne said under his breath, though he knew Balvinder could hear him. "Take her there."

Rapidly, like a stream merging into a single drop, the blue and silver light condensed into Balvinder's tall frame. Threads of it continued to whirl and quiver at the ends of his cloak and hair. Kayna was barely visible within his clutches, though her shrill, manic laughter echoed on as though trapped below the surface of water.

Thorne's dark gaze met Balvinder's piercing blue. A shared, fleeting grief passed between them.

She had fooled them both. It could never happen again.

Balvinder cast himself and Kayna into the erodosphere, a cyclonic spiral of opposites. Thorne was left alone on the curved roof. He took a few steps forward until his toes met the edge and he could look upon Emba's square.

The wails of the villagers lifted to the stars—despairing and accusatory. Thorne felt a sharp pang jolt through him. The mothers and fathers and siblings of the victims, they would never rest without wondering why, or how, or who. They were damned to ignorance—the cruelest curse. All blame would remain frozen, all sense of reason forever unattainable.

Pity sunk his knees to the shingle roof. He lifted his face to the night sky, the stars and moon illuminating every shadow caught there.

Release them from the impossible questions, he whispered to the Overseer, from the softest space in his mind. *And I will lift their chins above this sorrow.*

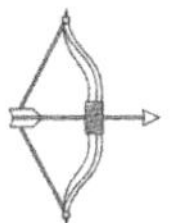

THORNE BOLTED TO HIS FEET THE MOMENT Balvinder fabricated behind him. He was not accustomed to others witnessing him on his knees, with the odd exception of more intimate circumstances. Even then, he preferred the way everything looked from above.

"It's done," Balvinder said, though his face was drawn and pale. "She will find it impossible to escape the bindings."

"No doubt she'll try her best," mused Thorne. "Particularly when we have to remove them for the Breathings."

Balvinder didn't respond. He was gazing down at the villagers. The entire square was teeming. Four people had begun to separate the bodies, while others sobbed or wailed or simply watched on through their fingers.

"She fooled us all," Thorne said, a mild attempt at consolation. "She knew you would follow her to Preo, to Nilah's family. But they were never her target."

Balvinder's gaze turned to frosted silver. "Yes, they were. Kayna set the raclor on Nilah's daughter, Blisse. Her husband Ansel and their child Zacharias—they were there too."

A weighted silence drew between them. Thorne smoothed his hair as he regarded Balvinder with a jaw so set that tendons jumped in his neck.

"The escaped raclor," he stated, more than asked.

Balvinder drew a heavy breath. "Yes."

"Did the raclor … did you get to them in time?"

Grief swelled behind Balvinder's eyes, and he averted them. "Come to my oasis," he said. "See for yourself."

Balvinder's oasis was set atop a higher plane of the Petrified Forest where the trees grew tall and lush, incongruent to their stony neighbours beyond the border. The branches drank in the light of the moon and a brilliant glow leaked from cracks in their trunks. A creek looped around the back, glittering at the base of the hill the house was set upon.

Thorne and Balvinder shifted nearby the front garden bed. White flowers sprung from it like snowflakes amidst periwinkle buds yet to bloom, all lining a row of expansive, panelled windows.

"He is still unconscious," Balvinder whispered as they entered the living room. The space was lit by trees entirely stripped of bark, their trunks coating the walls in a milky glow. "His wounds were severe."

"Who?" Thorne snapped.

Balvinder flashed him a warning look and strode ahead through the main hallway. Too often it felt as though he was cryptic for the sake of it. With an irritable huff, Thorne followed.

They stopped at the last room. Gently, Balvinder eased the door open with his fingertips before Thorne shouldered past him. Moonlight streamed through one window behind a single iron bed. Curled atop the blankets, facing away from the door with small, bare feet tucked in close—lay a child.

Blue light glimmered and sparked across his form; a translucent protective shell.

"The external wounds are mostly healed." Balvinder spoke in a hush. "But the bruising and broken bones will take more time."

Thorne stalked to the bed's end and peered around for a glimpse at the child's face. "Nilah's grandson," he observed. "Where is Blisse? And Ansel? Did Nilah not say they were camping together?"

Balvinder's mouth set in a firm line, and he only shook his head.

"I see," Thorne replied tersely. "You intervened, then."

"I found Zacharias at the very last moment. The raclor had already killed Blisse and Ansel."

"And? Where did it go?"

Balvinder wiped his brow. "It fled, so I brought the boy here, before you called me to Emba."

Thorne's expression was fierce. "You let it go?"

"He was dying."

"And now more may die," barked Thorne. "You should have gone after it."

Balvinder sighed and opened the door, motioning for them both to leave the room. Thorne threw his hands up and barged through to the hallway, jostling impatiently on his feet as Balvinder closed the door behind them.

They regarded each other for a stiff moment without speaking.

"I couldn't have left him there," Balvinder said at last.

Thorne rolled his eyes. "And what do you envisage will happen now?"

"Zacharias will need me. When he comes to, he will be lost."

"You plan to tell him the Truth?"

Balvinder hesitated. "Perhaps in parts."

"And that his dear grandmother is a bridge between human spirits and Essences he never knew existed?"

Another hesitation. Then—"He may not need to know about Nilah."

"He needn't know *any* of it," Thorne shot back.

"This wouldn't have happened if it weren't for our failings," Balvinder said quietly. "We failed to rescue the raclor, we failed to capture Kayna, and we failed to see through her games."

Thorne shook his head, each word a knife to every rigid layer of defensive skin he worked tirelessly to solidify.

"Perhaps some people are owed the Truth," Balvinder went on, gazing thoughtfully back at the door as though he could see the boy through it.

Biting his lip, Thorne fought hard not to persist with the argument. There was little point in it at this stage.

He suspected the situation would turn out much like Wade's. Over forty years ago, Nilah had raised Wade primarily at Balvinder's oasis. There was some irony in it, that a generation later, another Truth Insignia would be bestowed upon Nilah's bloodline through Balvinder's influence.

"I want nothing to do with it," Thorne said firmly. "Heal the boy if you must, but send him home once it's done. Too many scraggly ends are a threat, and we can't afford to have children poking around in the Truth. No matter who they're related to." He paused and crossed his arms. "Blisse and Ansel—where are their bodies?"

"I left them at the border of my oasis in my haste to save Zacharias. Soon I will take them to Preo, for Nilah's family to …" Balvinder trailed off, a watery sheen standing still in his eyes.

"To discover," Thorne finished for him. "Does Nilah know yet?"

Balvinder shook his head. "She is at Harlie's oasis awaiting an update on our progress."

"Well then," Thorne said smoothly. "Allow me to remain absent for that."

A soft call resounded beyond the door. "Mother?"

Thorne winced. The boy's voice struck him like a hot brand. Balvinder's face fell at the sound of it, his eyes turning grey.

With a sharp breath, Thorne turned on his heel, sorrow weighing every step—though he didn't let a trace of it show.

TWELVE

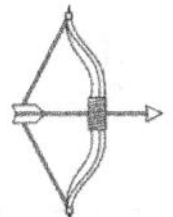

FROM THE HIGHEST POINT IN RYLORA, A TALL cylindrical structure utilised as a lookout tower, Thorne cast his gaze across the outdoor markets below. He enjoyed observing the wealthy folk trading there. They were always immaculately dressed and hugely self-important. The city was a well of Pride where Thorne could feel justly valued.

Two guards stood either side of the tower, clutching elaborately carved longbows with limbs of gleaming onyx. Attacks on Rylora tended to occur centuries apart, and even then they were easily thwarted. Thorne considered the job of the guards an admirable one, and yet vastly mundane between events where they were to be of any real use. At least they could look out upon a spectacular view.

The store Thorne was headed for was easy to spot down below, a gilded doorway nestled into the main street market. He spun into emerald waves and reappeared inside a room packed to bursting with various relics and lavish furniture. He strode past an older woman admiring a golden stool—right for the back wall, where plaques of gold, silver, copper and bronze were lined floor to ceiling.

Once he had selected a smooth golden plate, he carried it to the back where the shop owner was busying himself over a diamond-crusted watch. Thorne admired the piece for a moment. Those living on Ethra's western continent would never have laid eyes upon anything so extravagant. Preo traded in small quantities with Rylora, and in turn with Emba, but diamonds were hard to come by in those parts.

The shop owner was called to the main room by the woman inspecting the stool. Once he had disappeared from view, Thorne homed in on the tools strewn across the bench.

He had memorized every name, and whispered each under his breath.

Then he began to etch into the metallic surface of the plaque with a sharp-tipped metal pen. He worked swiftly, but his script was flawless.

Back when the Essences were instructed by the Overseer to put together the Chronicles—countless volumes recording the beginnings of free will and their part in it—Thorne had taken extra care with every word. Peirce's pessimistic rants were a *disaster*, he recalled, scrawled almost unintelligibly.

Balvinder and Westby were the only two who held a candle to what Thorne produced. You'd expect the Essence of Good to be good at something, after all. And Westby was all about Order and Efficiency.

Only nine Essences—Pride, Good, Evil, Pessimism, Optimism, Honesty, Desire, Obedience and Efficiency—and yet each had churned out multiple volumes for the Chronicles over the centuries. When he thought too deeply about it, Thorne resented the fact that his work was required to stand beside far less distinguished variations on the Truth. But it was there, nonetheless. And he was proud of it.

He completed the final name and slipped into the erodosphere with the plate held to his chest. He would be late—exactly as he had planned it. He despised sitting in wait, and always took pleasure in making an entrance.

The suite was a wing of Pacer Barlon's impressive guesthouse, to be used at Thorne's leisure. It was a gift from the ruler in thanks for his advisory.

Most times, Thorne wasn't there alone.

He appeared by the gilded mirror table and allowed his emerald Essence to whirl about him, uncovering his lean frame and raised chin with a little more flair than usual.

A single candle lit the high-ceilinged room and shone brightly against the pale green walls. Pearl-white marble wings swept along either side of the bed to hug a full moon at the headboard, with a crescent upheld at the foot.

Asha lay sprawled across the sheets in a strappy white dress, her long limbs iced in the light of the moon pouring in through the window. She watched Thorne carefully from a pair of mesmerizing, golden eyes, daring him closer.

Desire embodied—and what a body she was. Thorne raked his implacable gaze over every curve.

"Quite the entrance," Asha said in a hush, her voice like silk spilling over the softest skin. "I was beginning to think you had better things to do. But then I considered what might be superior to me, and I came up with nothing."

A smirk kinked Thorne's mouth. He set down the golden plate and approached the bed.

"What is that?" Asha raised a slender, jewel-bedecked finger to the plate.

"After," Thorne answered.

Asha's full lips curled as he knelt on the bed before her. A deep craving ached through the tangible and preternatural tapestry of his being. Not merely an ache to touch, but an ache to *be* touched. A side effect of his human form.

With deliberate slow movements for Asha's viewing pleasure, he pulled his cloak away. Then the shirt beneath it. His rippling torso carved itself out from the darkness, moonlight kissing each great bend of muscle.

He took a moment to gaze down at himself.

Asha's smooth dark legs curved around his knees. "Once you are done inspecting your own beauty, will you allow me to show you mine?"

Thorne smiled and cast his gaze again over Asha's form. But it was her eyes that gave him pause, glinting like gold jewels set into copper.

"Your eyes," he crooned. "Just beautiful."

Asha inclined her head. "Because they hold your reflection?" When Thorne only glowered down at her, she laughed—a tender, pretty sound—and a glimmer of affection crossed her otherwise bemused expression. "I jest. After all, the greatest misconception about you is that you take Pride only in yourself."

"Well, I *am* the most worthy of attention," Thorne replied, toying with the edge of her silk dress. "But yes." Tracing his thumb down to her knee, he paused on the thought. "There is beauty in all things, and often I feel I am the only one to see it."

"You are not as alone as you might think," Asha said, and something in her tone raised a scowl to Thorne's surface, though he took comfort in the words.

The moon was bright and sharp against the flat opal roofs of Rylora's otherwise rocky landscape. Asha and Thorne had shifted to the highest one, and she now rested between his legs with her back curled against his chest.

They had made love ten times over in Pacer Barlon's guesthouse.

Touching Asha often sent vivid shards of memory through Thorne's mind; flashes not of her, but of Harlie. He could still remember the feeling of her body against his—all hard edges and painfully strategic movements.

Unlike Asha—who spun like gold under his fingertips with her daring curves and fluent expertise—there wasn't a glimmer of passion to the act.

But even now, set up above the beauty of Rylora … he couldn't shake the thought of Harlie's critique. It was hundreds of years old now, and he had vastly improved in every capacity. He was sure of it. Yet in some unshakable way, he felt he could not rest soundly until the Essence of Honesty, of Truth, knew it too.

"Harlie mentioned that you've spoken of our … meetings," Thorne said. "All my so-called *practice*."

Asha huffed a laugh. "She inquired about us. So, I gave a glowing assessment." Thorne felt his unease fade a little at that. "It's difficult to lie in the face of Honesty," she added.

Harlie's newfound interest *was* perhaps an indication that Asha had painted him as desirable. Deciding to overlook the blatant disregard of his privacy, Thorne drew his arm around Asha and cupped her cheek, stroking its smooth, satin curve. "I do it all the time," he said.

Asha reached her hands back and touched the taut line of his jaw. "Your Pride yearns for affirmation," she said in a voice that melted against his ear.

Thorne said nothing, waiting for elaboration. As Desire in its purest form, Asha often knew how to make one feel as though they were strapped up and laid bare against a wall. Harlie was similar—only she threw knives and barely understood the impact, whereas Asha seemed to enjoy caressing the dark spaces Thorne wished she couldn't see.

"I give it freely, and so you return," she went on. "But you also desire the purest affirmation of the one who cannot colour Truth, don't you?"

Thorne snarled and something of a growl rose from his throat. She was right, and he resented her for voicing it. He could not help that he still desired Harlie's approval. The thought was infuriating. And that Asha knew it too … was unbearable.

"We imprisoned Kayna," he said, the stark shift in topic clanging in the silence that hung between them as Asha lowered her hands. "She possessed a raclor and set it on Nilah's daughter Blisse and her husband Ansel, and their son," Thorne fired on. "Then she slaughtered twenty children in Emba and piled their bodies in the square, where I found them."

Asha sat upright and pivoted to face him.

"Nilah's grandson, Zacharias, he was the only one to survive the raclor's attack. Blisse and Ansel were mutilated—Balvinder found them too late. But he has the boy at his oasis now and plans to nurture him back to health."

"You share this *now*?" Asha's face was poised at the crest of her shock. "Was this an attempt at catching me off guard for the most dramatic retelling possible?"

Thorne shrugged. "The dramatic is often unintentional with me," he said.

Asha slid away across the polished opal and sat up on her knees. "Where are you keeping Kayna?"

"Emba—in Raphe's old house," Thorne told her. "Balvinder bound her power to the chains, so she can't shift."

Asha sunk over her feet, her shimmering white dress on the opalescent roof giving the impression of a pearl on display in the centre of a clam. "And the possessed raclor?"

"Still loose," Thorne admitted, averting his eyes. "But Balvinder seems to think the boy is his priority."

Asha lowered her gaze to the glittering city beneath them. "Nilah will be devastated," she whispered.

Thorne pretended not to hear and cleared his throat. "There is something I must do," he said. "If you wish to meet again before the Breathing, return to the guesthouse in five days, at sunset."

"Forever demanding," Asha muttered. "But I will be here."

Thorne said nothing more. He shifted into emerald green and appeared again in the guesthouse bedroom.

Retrieving the golden plate from its place before the mirror, he hitched it under his arm and drew into the erodosphere, spinning like lightning back to Emba's heart.

THIRTEEN

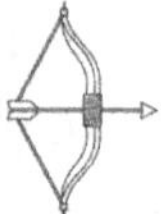

THE SQUARE WAS DEADLY QUIET. A COOL WIND rustled the pale leaves of the tree at its centre, which now hung over a space so empty it was as though the absence of the children lost could be felt just by standing in it.

Someone had positioned a stone at the trunk's base, twenty names carved laboriously into its surface. Thorne had seen it, memorised it, and etched the same names into the golden plate now clutched in his hands. Woven around the names was an ornate border with twenty tiny opals inlaid within.

He fixed the dedicatory piece over the stone with an adhesive tar he'd sent Colt to fetch earlier. Then he withdrew and paced backwards, angling his head at his handiwork. Nobody in Emba could have afforded such a dedication. It felt only proper that he assist where he could.

And he couldn't shake the feeling that the children wouldn't have died had he stopped the raclor, stopped Kayna, seen through her lies …

Thorne started. A figure had swept by him in his momentary attention lapse. A woman, clutching flowers. She sank before the tree and laid them down at the base of it. Then she seemed to register the plaque.

Thorne clenched his teeth and watched as she ran her fingers over each name, over letters inscribed by his hand. Her touch lingered over the second last. And then she wept.

Staring on, Thorne debated whether to stay or leave. The latter was tempting, but a pulsing energy kept him rooted to the spot.

Their bodies are temporary, he wanted to say. *But their spirits are eternal.*

The children would pass to the upper realm, nearer the Overseer. This was not their end. Only, she wouldn't know it until she reached hers.

He strode forward and extended his hand. His fingertips grazed the woman's shoulder and her racking sobs eased a little, her breaths coming more easily.

It wasn't often that he felt compelled to connect with a human spirit this way. Of course, most took in his Essence from the erodosphere to some degree, but to expose them to his most potent, tangible form … it wasn't permitted. But then, hadn't Kayna broken every set rule when she killed those children? And Gwin communicated often with Pacer Ketel of Maravier, and Peirce with many from the province of Thanron. They *all* did it.

With his hesitation alleviated, Thorne allowed his palm to rest against the woman's back. His skin turned to flaming tendrils of green light that seeped through her physical shell and right to the spirit that had dimmed inside her.

It was only possible to magnify what a human already desired. The woman clung to some shred of remaining Pride, it seemed. Perhaps in herself, or in the child taken from her.

Slowly, she rose to her feet. Wet tracks stained her cheeks but the sobs had ceased. Thorne pressed his other hand against her.

Lift your chin, sweetheart.

The woman looked right at him—through him. The soft command in her head. The unseen insistence. The force she would battle with upon waking every morning to be met with her child's absence. The Pride she would never see; only feel.

She took a breath and retreated along a dark side street, her chin lifted, and fiery emerald wisps stirring in her wake.

FOURTEEN

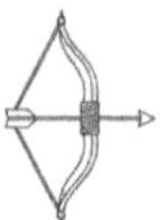

WHEN THORNE HEARD OF NILAH'S PLAN TO hold an assembly of the Essences, he volunteered his oasis as the meeting location. He enjoyed hosting the odd event—considered it a form of controlled socialisation. And there were few other places that compared to its grandeur.

Nilah arrived first, linked between Harlie and Asha as they shifted into the foyer in a flurry of cerise and amethyst light.

Thorne hurriedly adjusted his black coat, the gold stitching across its sleeves and collar glinting in the light of the torches atop intricate sconces lining the staircase.

His mouth pinched at the sight of his two lovers side by side—Harlie wearing slim trousers and a bell-sleeved shirt, and Asha in a fitted, cream dress draped in lace.

Ivory and ebony. Cutting edges and sensual curves.

Harlie's hair fell just past her shoulders in natural sandy waves, whilst Asha's was styled into a black braid and wound into an elaborate bun. They were each beautiful, and yet as starkly different as night was from day.

"Thank you for sharing your home with us, Thorne," Nilah said. He cut his gaze to her, realising that in the wake of the other two, he'd hardly registered her state. She looked a mess; her skin wan and taut, wearing the same dress as he'd last seen her in, a veil of grief over her typically vibrant demeanor.

"You look terrible," he said.

Harlie laughed sharply. "I thought I was the Honest one."

Nilah's expression remained unchanging, and her voice came out flat and muted. "Kayna killed my daughter and her husband, and mauled my grandson," she said. "Terrible is likely a very kind analysis, and hardly adequate for describing how I feel."

"Understandably," Asha said softly, her jewelled fingers glittering as she swept Nilah's hair from her face. "You are safe from her now—your family too."

"Until the Breathing," murmured Nilah, fear tinting her wide green eyes a darker shade. "We'll have to free her for that."

"She won't lay a finger on you," Thorne declared, descending the staircase and stopping right before her. "I will make sure of it."

He expected gratitude, but Nilah simply stared at him, her gaze hollow.

"There is no sufficient comfort to alleviate this sort of grief," Harlie said, her tone frank rather than accusatory. "The damage has been done."

A loud clatter sounded from the dining room to their right. "Damn," came the dreariest voice ever to grace Ethra's soundscape. Or rather, to curse it. "Damn the sun and the moon and the stars and all that shines—"

"Ah," Asha sighed. "Just what we needed."

Thorne let a heavy sigh guide him into the adjacent room, where Peirce was straightening a fallen chair. He looked up through a mess of greasy, black hair as Thorne cleared his throat.

"Why is it that I seem to gravitate toward the most inconvenient space?" Peirce inquired, mostly to himself.

"Beats me," Thorne replied, striding forward to correct the chair's position. "Where is your perky little opposite?"

Peirce laughed, if you could call it that—it was more of an impassive, dissonant bark. "Caught up sniffing flowers in Maravier, I'd say."

Thorne allowed himself a smile. Though eternally Pessimistic, Peirce was probably right. He spent the most time with Gwin out of all the Essences, despite their evident differences. Or perhaps it was more accurate to say that Gwin forced herself upon him more so than the rest of them.

"Let's take our seats," Thorne called back into the foyer. "The others shouldn't be far off." Asha strode in first and cast him a faint smile as she sat at the square, oak table. Harlie had her arm hooked in Nilah's and guided her to a chair. It was as though the Melder had aged ten years overnight, Thorne thought with a pang.

The space above the table wavered and a sliver of yellow gold melted across the oak. Optimism shone out in a bursting ray of sun as Gwin formed, cross-legged under tumbling white-blonde hair and an ever-fresh complexion. She beamed brightly around at Nilah and the Essences.

"Is that really necessary, Gwin?" Thorne inquired with an arched brow, eyeing her bare feet on his table.

"I was aiming for the front door!" she trilled, clambering down into the chair beside Pessimism. "And sorry I'm late. I was held up in the Maravier gardens." Through his stringy, matted hair, Peirce shot Thorne a look that said—*told you.*

"How lovely to see you all," Gwin gushed on. "I always enjoy meeting between Breathings. I mean, they're compulsory, but it's not often that we get to simply—"

"This isn't a social gathering," Thorne interjected. "We are here to discuss Kayna's captivity."

Gwin inclined her head, the smile on her face faltering only slightly. "Captivity?"

Two of the remaining chairs suddenly filled. In a puff of glistening umber, Colt sat rigid in one of them, his mousey brown hair a little frazzled around his temples.

Westby occupied the other, dusting red wisps from his shoulder. His auburn hair was tied away from his face and he wore a white shirt with a collar that boasted a design of fine, black stitching. Westby was labelled many things—as Thorne was, as they all were—though he preferred the term *Efficiency*.

"Perhaps you should take shifting lessons from these two," Thorne suggested to Gwin, waving a hand at Obedience and Efficiency, both straight-backed and alert.

"What a fun prospect," Gwin mused.

"Everyone is already here," Colt said nervously. "You said eleven, didn't you Thorne? It is eleven exactly, it is."

"We arrived a little early," Harlie said.

Colt's gaze darted around the table. "I'm not late," he clarified. "You said eleven."

Thorne rolled his eyes. "Nobody is accusing you of tardiness, Colt. Calm yourself."

"Nilah," Westby murmured, gazing across at the Melder. "I am deeply sorry to hear of your loss."

"Loss?" Gwin's attention snapped from one face to the other. "What loss?"

"Thank you, Westby," Nilah said, though the words slipped from her lips as nothing more than a whisper.

"Balvinder won't be attending the meeting," Westby went on. "I visited his oasis and heard the story from him yesterday. He wishes to stay with Zacharias, and has asked if you, Thorne, will lead the discussion."

"How is he?" Nilah straightened a little in her chair, the faintest flicker of light returning to her eyes. "Zacharias?"

"Quite well," replied Westby. "The broken bones are mending slowly but surely. I didn't speak with him directly. Balvinder has requested that the rest of us maintain our distance. He doesn't wish to overwhelm the boy with a colourful pack of disembodied voices."

Nilah nodded gravely. "And he hasn't told Zacharias about me? What I do?"

"No." Westby's already fine lips grew thinner. "And he will not. He thinks it best to minimise what Truth Zacharias knows."

"Finally he's speaking *some* sense," murmured Thorne. "But there's more to this than the boy. Allow me to share the whole story …"

Nilah stared at the wall as Thorne recounted the discovery of the possessed raclor, its escape, the failed attempt at cornering Kayna, the raclor's attack on Nilah's family, the slaughter in Emba, and Kayna's final imprisonment.

While Thorne spoke, a thread of orange snaked across the table to wind around Nilah's taut, white fist. It came from Peirce, who was studying her from behind his tangle of hair with the deepest, darkest sort of empathy crystalising in his eyes.

Gwin's yellow followed, then Colt's russet, Westby's red, Harlie's fuchsia, Asha's mauve—even Thorne allowing an emerald tendril to slip free as he spoke—until Nilah was clutching all seven pulsating colours.

When the report came to an end, the Essences withdrew, and Gwin spoke into the eerie silence left behind. "Oh goodness," she murmured. "Oh, Nilah." She rose from her chair and stood behind the Melder, taking her ash-blonde hair between her fingers and beginning to braid it. "You mustn't allow this to consume your joy. It isn't your fault, or Balvinder's, or Thorne's. It's Kayna's and only Kayna's. And Zacharias—he will be fine under Balvinder's care. You know that better than anyone."

Nilah's eyes fluttered to close and she drew a deep breath through her nose while Gwin plaited her hair. Thorne's dark expression softened. At its worst, Gwin's Optimism was a nightmare. But she had her more tender moments.

"We know it's Kayna's fault," he said, snapping back to the matter at hand. "That's why she is the one in chains."

"Here's to hoping they hold," Asha murmured, her full lips twisting.

"I'm always impressed by how you keep this place." Westby cast his gaze about the room, the fireplace swept clean, the hanging chandelier, every surface spotless.

"He had me over to clean it yesterday," interposed Colt. Thorne glared at him. It was true—Colt was useful when a mundane task was in order.

"What good is the Essence of Obedience if he isn't given abundant opportunities to *obey*?" Thorne posed, folding his arms as if to mark his stance.

"That isn't how it works," Harlie said, becoming the next recipient of Thorne's simmering stare. Though she wasn't fazed. "Colt doesn't exist for you to order around."

"Enough of that," Asha smoothly intervened. "Has the Overseer spoken to anyone?"

Silence held around the table.

"Then we must assume He is pleased with Kayna's captivity—that He approves of it," Westby murmured, dragging his slender fingers across his chin.

"Yes," Nilah said softly, and seven pairs of eyes went to her. "Having Kayna run rampant is no longer an option. I do believe if the Overseer held issue with that, He would make it known."

The following hour involved loud and heated discussions about how they might transport Kayna to the Breathing House every second month.

"Balvinder can handle her," Westby said.

"No," Thorne objected. "We will all lay hands on her while we shift, *and* throughout the Breathing. It's far too risky to leave her to her own devices, even for so much as a split-second."

"This is a disaster," was Peirce's helpful seed of input.

"The Overseer might help us," Gwin suggested.

And so the assembly of Essences drew to an end with the mostly conclusive decision to shift Kayna *collectively* to the Breathing House when the time came.

As they all rose from their chairs, Westby motioned for Nilah to join him by the fire.

"Allow me to find you something exquisite to wear for the next Breathing," Thorne heard him say.

Nilah laughed softly without humour. "I've barely thought about clothes since …" she trailed off, and Westby dusted the shoulder of her dress.

"You must carry on," he said. "You must carry on because you have learnt that the dark is only a shade over the day, and you can choose which to see."

Tears spilled down her cheeks as she gazed up at the face of Stability, Order, Competence, Efficiency. Though he preferred the latter, Westby was all those things and more, one quality shaped around multiple manifestations. Perhaps he sensed that he was what Nilah needed this particular night.

Thorne turned quickly away to avoid witnessing any more of her despair—and spun right into Harlie.

She stood rigid, watching him with a curious tilt of her head as he worked to hide his surprise.

"Yes?" he said brusquely.

"If I am being honest with you—"

"Which you always are …"

"I must admit that I have missed your company," she said. "And would like the opportunity to assess your progress after all these—"

"Shut *up*," Thorne hissed, taking her by the elbow to a corner of the room. He threw a glance at Asha, who was speaking with Peirce in the foyer. Colt and Gwin had shifted away already.

He turned on Harlie. "Do me the courtesy of lowering your voice," he growled. "And if you use the word *progress* one more time …"

Harlie simply smiled—a sharp, rapid gesture. "Progress is inevitable, isn't it?"

Thorne pointed a finger at her nose before flicking it. Upon second thought he wondered if the gesture was too playful, and corrected himself by applying adequate amounts of acid to his next words. "What did I just say?"

"All right, calm your flaming Pride." Harlie spoke now in a hush. Thorne couldn't help but like the way her voice sounded in a whisper. The hard edge of it rounded back to something more tender, even if the words were not. "What do you make of what I said?"

Thorne bristled, dormant nerves coming alive under his skin. The invitation was flattering, yes. But he was not sure he could stomach another critique. Of course he hoped to prove himself, but what if the outcome wasn't satisfactory? Harlie would voice it, openly. He might never speak to her again.

"I feel it might be a dangerous game," he admitted, as there was little he could hide from Honesty itself.

He recalled Asha's words from a few nights prior; that he desired a pure sort of affirmation only Harlie could offer. He didn't like to be thought of as desperate, or in need of something he himself couldn't provide.

Thorne was self-sufficient in all things, and he would not grovel for Harlie's affection or analysis. "I will see you in Emba before the next Breathing," he said stiffly, though a part of him imagined guiding her to his bed. He quickly banished the thought. "We are a complex pairing, and I can't say I desire complexity at this time."

"You and I are complex by our very nature," Harlie retorted, raising her chin a little. *So why not?*—it seemed to say. The movement was so minimal in its defiance, and yet it touched Thorne's core like nothing else she'd ever said or done.

He swallowed hard and forbad himself to falter. "Goodnight, Harlie."

⇒——————→

Thorne passed by Asha and Peirce on his way to the front door. "Don't break anything on your way out," he said, mostly to Peirce.

His gaze met Asha's for a fleeting moment. He remembered suggesting another meeting with her in five days' time, their usual arrangements in Rylora. And he might've reminded her of it, had Harlie not remained in the dining room, her lucid green eyes searing holes into his back.

"Westby," he said, casting a sideline glance at the fireplace. "You will shift Nilah back to Preo?"

"Of course," Westby said. Nilah was no longer crying, Thorne noted. Good.

With the remaining Essences still loitering in his home, he strode out into the night. Hopefully they'd be gone by the time he returned.

He'd never liked goodbyes. Even the simplest, most insignificant of them. Occasionally he wondered if the others felt the same, or if it was an imperceptible facet of his Essence alone that brought forward the discomfort. He dared not ask, for fear that it might be perceived as some sort of tragic weakness.

His thoughts trailed to Harlie—the fractional tilt of her chin as she'd attempted to challenge his reluctance. Asha, whose golden eyes threatened to swallow him whole if he looked too closely at them.

A wind flecked with ice crystals swept along the coast. Though the weather in Ethra had been relatively pleasant that day, it could change in an instant. Earth was said to be different; its conditions less severe. The existence of the Essences in their most potent forms seemed to disrupt Ethra's weather cycle. The metaphysical upsetting the tangible.

Thorne yanked his coat further around himself, ducking his nose behind the high collar. Perhaps it would snow overnight. He hoped so.

When the cliffs were coated in fresh white powder and the waves had iced the rocky coast, Thorne could appreciate the spectacle from the windows of his oasis, or pack on his warmest coats and boots to forge a path through it.

He adored the way a landscape could reset itself so wholly and suddenly. It was one thing, and yet it could be many.

Tonight the starlit sky punctured the sea with its dazzling reflection of a crisp half-moon.

Making his way to the edge of the nearest cliff and his favourite vantage point, Thorne allowed the wind to whip his ebony hair out of place. He came to a halt at the very edge of the cliff, peering down at the waves churning below.

He thought of Nilah and her weeping eyes, bloodshot and hollow. After all that went on, how would she cope with the next Breathing? He wondered. Simply seeing Kayna again would shake her, no doubt.

And in the meantime, her grandson Zacharias … the boy was bound to learn a portion of Truth under Balvinder's care. Thorne hoped Balvinder would reveal nothing more than his own voice. Even *that* much was excessive.

But the boy wasn't his problem. There was a raclor to catch—loose and unhinged. He would find it, even if that meant looking under every rock and delving into every cave in Ethra. He would find it himself, without any assistance, and it would pay for what it did to Nilah. As would Kayna.

Thorne faced the sea and allowed his mind to drift and his eyes to close as the wind whistled around him.

Then he tilted on his feet—and fell forward over the cliff.

An instinctively human elation rippled through his body. The sensation seized his chest and throat and roared madly in his ears. The drop was significant, but he knew it well enough to accurately time his shift.

A few feet before he was to meet the rocks, he burst into green light and spun out across the water.

He remembered once—back when Nilah had first accepted her duty as the Melder—she had asked whether his existence as an Essence ever felt lonely. Often he thought of her words; mulled them over.

It was a strange question, really. Loneliness was not simply dictated by the absence of company.

One was required to thoroughly enjoy their own company before seeking additional avenues of friendship. And Thorne did.

He was untouchable. Proud. Powerful.

Frost melted in the wake of his lustrous form. He rushed against the icy wind and erupted upward, allowing his angular features to form at the crest of his vapour. Through his nose he drew a long breath; drank the cold night air and salty sea mist.

No—he would never be lonely. He was pivotal, and desired by almost every living thing. His place in the universe was magnificent and sure.

As he glided toward the stars, he basked in the steadfast Truth of it.

ACKNOWLEDGEMENTS

A huge thank you to the readers, family members and friends who have supported the release of Essence and spurred on this novella in the process. You are the driving force when my own wants to curl up and hide.

Thank you mother dearest for all that you do. For working through draft after draft, listening to my never-ending ramblings, and making this journey far less solitary.

Thank you *grandmother* dearest for your efforts with this novella. I can't say how much I appreciate your insights and incredibly acute, literary eye.

Gabriella Bujdosó—I am in constant awe of your enthusiasm and everything you produce. Thank you for the stunning cover art. Your talent is *exceptional* and I can't wait to see more from you.

Wictoria Nordgård—your illustrations and our ongoing dialogue has triggered greater clarity and a well of inspiration for Ethra and its characters. You are a beauty and I'm so glad we connected.

And to the readers who have been awaiting this novella—thank you for all the shared excitement and kind words. It makes all the difference.

HAYLEY GABRIELLE IS A MELBOURNE-BASED writer of mostly fantasy and science fiction. She has seen works published across a range of journals and anthologies worldwide, and recently won the 2018 Alan Marshall Short Story Award. *Essence* marks the release of her debut young adult fantasy series, *The Essence Chronicles*, paving the way for her longer works of fiction.

To keep up to date with Hayley's latest releases,
subscribe at
www.hayleygabrielle.com

or follow **@hayleygabriellewriter** on Instagram
for updates on future releases.